RUSTKILLER

BOOKS BY DEAN F. WILSON

THE CHILDREN OF TELM

The Call of Agon
The Road to Rebirth
The Chains of War

THE GREAT IRON WAR

Hopebreaker
Lifemaker
Skyshaker
Landquaker
Worldwaker
Hometaker

THE COILHUNTER CHRONICLES

Coilhunter
Rustkiller
Dustrunner

HIBERNIAN HOLLOWS

Hibernian Blood
Hibernian Charm

A COILHUNTER CHRONICLES NOVEL

RUSTKILLER

DEAN F. WILSON

Cover illustration by Duy Phan

First Edition 2017

ISBN 978-1-909356-21-4

DIOSCURI PRESS

Published by Dioscuri Press
Dublin, Ireland

www.dioscuripress.com
enquiries@dioscuripress.com

Welcome to the Wild North

CONTENTS

Chapter

Chapter One

NOT THAT WAY

The way the Coilhunter put his boot down in the sand told you a lot. It told you he meant business. It told you that business meant only one of you was getting out alive. It told you he meant it to be him.

"Stick 'em up or I'll shoot 'em down," the Coilhunter said. He had the pistol ready, and almost a clean shot. The shooting might have been clean, but the killing wasn't.

Strawman Sanders stood across the way, far enough that you couldn't see the twitching of his fingers or the sweat on his brow, but close enough that he could see the Coilhunter's grim eyes beneath the brim of his cowboy hat, and that metal mask beneath, covering his mouth, hiding the smile.

"You've got the wrong man, Nox," Sanders shouted back from the side of his mouth, keeping a piece of straw like a cigar in the other. You never saw him without it. He must've chewed through a whole wheat field by now. No one knew where he got it though. There wasn't any farmland for miles.

"Let's talk it through then," the Coilhunter replied.

"I ain't talkin' to no gun o' yours, Nox."

"You talk to me," the Coilhunter said, pointing to himself with the gun, "or you talk to the sand, and then the worms."

"I had nothin' to do with that robbery," Sanders said. "It was a setup. Ask Lawless Lyle. He's been leadin' the crime lords 'round these parts. I wasn't a part o' it. I was just there lookin', keepin' my own business."

The Coilhunter coughed, letting a puff of black smoke filter out of his mask. "Just there lookin' and keepin' your own business," he repeated. "Sounds like you might've been just there watchin' and robbin' at the same time too."

"I swear, Nox. I ain't no robber. I earned my way fair and square."

"Fair and square," the Coilhunter mused. He'd heard a lot of that over the years. If fair was beating a shopkeeper black and blue, then sure. If square was shooting someone because they looked at you the wrong way, then double sure.

"Made it in the mines," Sanders said.

"Funny, that," the Coilhunter rasped. "Red-hide Zeke worked in the mines. And he ended up dead, with not a thing on 'im. Now, I know it's hot out here. Why, it's positively roastin'. But I ain't heard of no one takin' off everything they own, not least their prized weddin' ring."

If Strawman Sanders wasn't already sweating, he would be now, and it'd have nothing to do with the sun.

"Now, tell me," the Coilhunter continued, "what's that there I see on your fat finger?"

Sanders' hand trembled. "This? Oh, it's … it's just my own weddin' band."

"Now, why do you have to go and lie, Sanders? Last I heard, you'd not been tamed yet."

"Well, since then—"

"Let me finish. Ya see, last I heard was yesterday, and that was from good old Honest Pete. Now, you know Pete. Everyone in this God-damn desert knows Pete. No one's got a bad word to say about 'im, and that's sayin' a lot 'round these parts. You tellin' me Honest Pete's a liar?"

Sanders struggled with his words, barely making an audible sound at all. When he'd finally choked himself up entirely, perhaps to save the Coilhunter from doing the job himself, he pressed his lips together firmly. If you were digging yourself into a hole by talking, then you'd better shut up quick.

The Coilhunter's stare was terrifying. His hat cast a shadow over his dark eyes. "Now, I ain't no bettin' man, but if I were, I'd say your fat finger and Red-hide Zeke's rottin' one have a little somethin' in common."

Still Sanders clenched his mouth. The piece of straw shuddered there.

"Now, is that just lookin' and keepin' your own business, or did ya keep a little somethin' of his as well?"

The panic was rising in Sanders, but he tried not to show it. They all tried not to show it, but the Coilhunter saw it all the same.

"Is this what ya mean by 'fair and square'?" Nox asked.

He wanted Sanders to break, to fall to his knees,

to own up, and rat out whoever else was in on it. Lawless Lyle was in hiding, and he needed a way to get to him. Sanders was that way. Nox didn't really want him dead. He wanted him squealing.

But Sanders ran. Maybe in his mind, he thought that was the wise thing to do, but the Coilhunter made a living out of gunning down people who ran. You couldn't outrun justice, not if it was him.

Nox had a clear shot, and had no quarrels with shooting bad men in the back, but he wasn't so sure Strawman Sanders was altogether bad. Mixed up with the wrong people, sure, but not bad. If Nox killed everyone who was in with the wrong crowd, there'd be no one left in the Wild North.

So the Coilhunter chased him instead.

It was your lucky day if there was a bounty on your head and the Coilhunter chased you with his boots instead of his bullets. A few of the Wanted even escaped that way. Sanders must've realised it, because he gave it hell when he ran, for fear he'd be going there soon himself.

Sanders kicked up a fury of dust in his wake, and the Coilhunter darted through the haze, shielding his eyes with the brim of his hat, while the filter on his mask took care of the rest. If his prey didn't dive down a dune and race up the next one, he might have fired a grappling hook his way, and so reel him in slow and steady, like a desert fish. Instead, he had to hound him fast and frenzied.

They were nearing the wastelands, that empty stretch of land where the sun was blotted out by the tremendous scrapyard walls of the Rust Valley. It was flat and featureless there, with nowhere to hide, but everywhere to run. You could keep on running, right until your legs buckled or your heart gave out, or your body went into shock from the sudden shift from boiling heat to freezing cold. Nox smiled inside his mask. He knew he'd got him.

Or so he thought.

They say everyone's got a surprise hidden in them, that we've all got one card we've never shown before. Sometimes we never play it. And sometimes, like when you're being chased by the Coilhunter, you rip that card out of your sleeve real quick.

Strawman Sanders turned sharply, abandoning the route towards the wastelands and heading towards the winding passages of the Rust Valley itself. The idea of it was crazy. If you got a hand with that in it, you'd go and fold like lightning. You wouldn't keep on playing. You wouldn't keep on betting.

But Strawman Sanders felt he had nothing to lose. Funny, that. He had his life.

The scrapyard jungle opened up before them. The walls towered high with bashed-up vehicles, some for civilians, many more for the war, that endless war that touched every part of Altadas but the lawless north. It's where old cars went to die. And you let them. You didn't go in after them.

"Not in there!" Nox shouted over as Sanders vanished into the metal maze.

Sanders didn't listen. You could risk your life in the Rust Valley or guarantee death outside with the Coilhunter. It wasn't like Nox was known for mercy. But Nox knew that the clockwork constructs in the

Rust Valley weren't known for it either.

Nox ran to the unmarked gate leading into that vehicle graveyard. He halted fast, skidding in the sand. Part of him felt like running in, not just to catch Strawman Sanders, but to pull him out, to save him from that horrid fate that awaited him. There was only one person who was said to have come out of the Valley alive, and not all of him came out. For the Coilhunter, there were few places in the Wild North he considered off limits, and this was one of them. Hell, it was bang smack at the top of the list.

He heard a cry, a shriek of pain, followed by the sound of grinding steel. Instinct pushed him on, right between those endless walls of junk. He ran in, guns ready, not entirely sure what good they'd do. He peered around a corner, spotting Strawman Sanders' body on the ground, and something leaning over it, something not quite right, something that wasn't human. It was a clockwork construct. They were all different, made up of mismatching parts. This one had five legs, and something like a head, and something like a blade for an arm. It was shredding Sanders one strip at a time.

Nox didn't know what to do. Then Sanders' head lolled to one side, his eyes almost popping. He gave that awful look the Coilhunter'd seen many times before. That look of begging to be put out of his misery. The clockwork construct would do it, sure enough, but it was taking its damn time. Some said they hated humans like the Coilhunter hated the sun. That was why you didn't go in there, why you left them to themselves. That was why you prayed that's all they'd do, that they'd never come out.

Sanders' eyes made that eternal plea. By rights, the Coilhunter should've made this his final lesson. He owed that man nothing. That man owed Redhide Zeke a lot. But something gnawed at Nox, like that clockwork construct gnawed at Sanders' skin. He pointed his pistol around the corner, aiming at Sanders' head, and fired.

Sanders went out cold. That was the good part.

The bad part was when the clockwork construct turned to look at Nox, spotting not just flesh on him, but metal to scavenge as well. It didn't see the Coilhunter's jaw drop behind his mask, but it did see the flash of fear in his eyes.

He ran, back out through the entrance. The clockwork construct followed, chasing him out into the desert like he'd just chased Strawman Sanders. The Coilhunter hoped to God, and maybe even the Devil as well, that he wouldn't end up just as dead.

Chapter Two

SAND AND STEEL

Nox bolted over the dunes, while the clockwork construct clambered after him. It didn't so much as run as throw itself forward, landing on its unsteady legs, before dragging itself on a little more in preparation for the next leap. The Coilhunter heard the metal clang and the sand spray high. He also heard the leather of his own gear squeak as he scarpered through the sands, like a little muted cry for help.

He thought by now the creature should have slowed and turned. It wasn't supposed to come out this far. This wasn't its territory. Yet the lust for blood and rivets was on its iron tongue. Nox thought that maybe it'd chase him to the ends of the earth, and maybe even beyond.

In the flurry of footfalls, the Coilhunter didn't notice a rock barely covered by the dust. He tripped over it, bracing himself as he fell. He tried to scramble up, but the clockwork construct was already upon him, stabbing and slashing. He saw two pronged legs to the right of his head, and one to the left. There was a clang as the creature's bladed arm stabbed at his back, striking the reinforced steel plating of the guitar that was strapped there. That was a good thing and a bad thing. It helped keep the Coilhunter alive, but if there was one thing these constructs lusted for more than anything, it was metal.

It paused for a moment. It must've been wondering what it would do with the metal. Maybe it'd make itself another stabbing arm, or perhaps another leg to give it better stability.

Nox couldn't turn around, or it'd slice through his flesh, casting away his carcass as it dug for metal. The clockwork constructs didn't so much want to tear you apart as consider you in the way of their goal. Maybe there was a bit of metal in your belly. You'd think they would have learned by now that they wouldn't find it there, but they kept on searching.

Nox tried to crawl away on his elbows, but the stabbing blade came down on his back, dinting the steel plating, pinning him in place. It seemed to have spotted the metal tank there too, filled with everything the Coilhunter needed to breathe. He wondered what he'd have to do to get away. Maybe he'd have to gnaw off an arm or leg. Maybe it'd do it for him.

He reached for his right pistol. It'd do no good. These bullets wouldn't pierce metal. He couldn't fight this thing. He had to run.

They say necessity is the mother of all inventions, and Nox was a bit of an inventor himself. It dawned on him that maybe the creature, which still inspecting the metal on his back, would like the metal of his gun. He tapped the barrel off one of its metal legs, letting the clang echo out. It halted, moving its odd head down towards the sound. Nox flicked open the barrel, letting it spin and click multiple times. The construct flinched, raising its bladed arm in defence. Nox gave it another flick, casting the bullets out into the sand farther away. Then he threw the gun itself as far as he could.

The clockwork construct got up off him and scurried over to the bullets first, collecting them together in a neat little pile. Then it moved about, looking for the gun. Nox hated the blowing sands most times, but now they helped. The gun was half-buried. Nox couldn't help but think that he might be as well soon enough.

He tried to crawl away slowly. He spotted the creature turning, so he froze. No matter how brave you were, sometimes you had to play dead. It sure beat the real thing. It turned back to its search, and Nox scrambled away again. He was debating how far he should crawl before he got up to run. He needed distance. He needed the construct not to notice.

But it noticed.

It glanced at him and gave out a sharp, mechanical cry, like metal grinding against metal.

Nox got up and ran. The creature raced after him. This time, Nox used his other pistol, firing back towards it. The bullets pinged off the surface, bouncing away. The creature looked at them as it passed, slowing a little. It'd be back to scavenge those, no doubt.

Nox pressed several buttons on a tracking device on his left wrist. They didn't seem to do anything. If he wasn't running for his life, he might have been able to check why. This was a bad time not to be able to call for backup.

The creature was almost upon him. Nox couldn't run any more. He knew he had to fight. With what, he had no idea. He halted and turned fast. The creature halted too, surprised. Maybe it wasn't used to its prey fighting back. As a bounty hunter, Nox was well used to that.

Nox reached his hand up slowly to his back, unstrapping the guitar. His finger grazed a string, sounding out a note. The clockwork construct cocked its head, curious. Pity it was so curious about his insides too. Nox held the guitar up, showing the metal plating on the back, letting the sun beam off it. That damn sun was like a spotlight when it came to metal. It conspired with everything to kill you, even something as unnatural as a clockwork construct.

Nox held the guitar up by the fingerboard, resting his thumb against a button on the side. Just as the creature was about to pounce, he pressed it and lobbed the guitar towards it. It reached out for it, but it couldn't quite see it, because the guitar sprayed out a thick plume of smoke.

The Coilhunter vanished into the haze. He could've tried to run again, but he would have been running out into the open, out to where it'd find him. And besides—he liked that guitar. He didn't quite feel like leaving it behind.

He circled around the creature in the smoke. He was used to this, stalking his own prey through the smog of a city, or the self-induced smog of his gadgets. The construct wasn't used to it, however, and didn't seem to know what to do. That was just how

Nox liked it.

Nox aimed his right arm towards its head, priming the grappling hook launcher. He fired, letting the hook grab on to the creature's neck. The coiling wire tugged him up onto the construct's back. It roared and reared, bucking like a mechanical horse. Nox held on tight to the reins.

He felt around with his left hand, looking for wires, or springs, or whatever it was that made these creatures work. Some said they needed a mate to power them up, that they worked like clockwork, so they had to keep on winding. Nox was curious about that, but he was a lot more interested in how to tear them apart.

He pulled a dagger from his belt and stabbed wildly at the creature's neck. He couldn't quite see or feel wires, but there were all sorts of parts in there, chugging away. There were a lot of little ticking noises. He dug in deep, shovelling out some of the parts. The construct screamed and turned about, trying to shake him off. It couldn't quite reach towards its back. Funny, that. It didn't like someone stabbing it from behind either.

Nox kept going, even though he didn't quite know what he was doing. He knew it was working though, as the construct became sluggish, slumping to the ground. It twitched and moaned, but the movements became slighter, and the sounds lower. Eventually, as the smoke faded, the creature was dead—if machines could die.

Nox clambered off it and grabbed his guitar. It looked a lot more battered than usual. He was used to people firing at him, and using that metal plating like a shield, but boy was he not used to this.

He was about to walk away when he noticed something like a mechanical heart in the construct's chest. He wondered if that was its power source, keeping it ticking. He took some tools from his belt and unscrewed the device. It was a lot of cogs and pieces. That was right up his alley as a toymaker and a mechanic. Some kids said they wanted a construct as a pet, but that was one hell of a dangerous toy. It'd be right at home in the Coilhunter's collection.

"Well," Nox said, looking down at the metal ruin. "I hope I never see your kind again."

He walked off, casting the metal heart up and down in his hand. If only there was a Wanted poster for that.

Chapter Three

THE SEA OF SORROWS

It took a long while to fix the tracker on his wrist, and far longer to wait for his monowheel to arrive. The sun was beating down bad, taking advantage of the situation, hoping to take one more sucker out before the night got it too.

Nox drove to the nearest rum-hole, the so-called Sea of Sorrows, a ramshackle establishment that was a bit too close to the Rust Valley. You'd think no one'd make that trek out there, but then here was Nox, tired and thirsty. The others at the bar weren't there for bounties. They were there for the moonshine and the sundazzle, the kind of stuff that burned real hot and knocked you out cold.

No one flinched when he entered. Normally they would, but everyone there was too far soaked. Maybe they saw four of him, but it seemed more likely they weren't seeing much at all.

Only the barman, Swill Roberts, seemed surprised.

"H-h-howdy," he said, straightening up his waistcoat. "I hope you're not here for t-trouble. We're an ace-high establishment here, so we are. Even got the registration." He pointed to a warrant on the wall from the Good Gullet Gang, which marked him as an "authorised trader," under their protection.

Nox shrugged. "Well, you ain't under mine." He pulled out a stool and sat down. "But I'm not here for trouble." He pointed towards the bottles of whiskey stacked neatly on the shelf behind. "I'm here for that."

The relief was visible on Swill Roberts' puckered face. He fumbled with a glass, then paused. "You sure you wouldn't want something … stronger?"

Nox looked at the men on either side of him, most of them face-down on the bar. He clutched the hair of one, lifting up his head just enough to see the drool, then let him collapse back down again.

"I might be here to drown my sorrows, but I don't wanna drown myself as well."

"As you like," Swill Roberts said, filling up the glass with his finest whiskey. You could tell it was his finest by how high up it was, and by the ornate bottle. It took him a while to get the cork out. It must've been a long time in there. "Wet your whistle on that, Nox, and tell me it isn't the desert oasis."

Nox lifted up his mask, shielding the scars on his face, and had a quick sip. The burn was a soothing kind, unlike the burn of everything else in the desert. It felt good to have a glass in his hand instead of always having a gun.

"That's somethin' fine all right," Nox said.

Swill Roberts smiled and topped up the glass. "Rough day, huh?"

"Yeah." Though it wasn't quite as bad as the day Strawman Sanders had.

"Out catching bad guys, I'd wager."

"Well, that ain't much of a wager, now, is it?"

"You won't find any in here, at least. Too drunk to do any bad."

"Too drunk to do any good either."

"We can't all be bounty hunters."

Nox forced a smile, forgetting that the barman couldn't see it. "Yeah. Someone has to be hunted."

He pulled back his mask again, taking a larger gulp. He noticed Swill Roberts watching his every twitch, staring at his hand as he gripped the glass, watching it like a gunslinger. There were some who came up with the codes you live by out here in the wild, but someone must've gunned them down before they got to write them up. One of those rules was that you always drank with your gun hand, to show you weren't planning anything funny. But for the Coilhunter, well, both hands were his gun hands, so you never knew what he was planning. Chances are, though, he was planning your death.

But someone had already died that day, and maybe he wasn't supposed to. Nox still had the poster of Strawman Sanders in his pocket, all crumpled up. Normally he'd drag the body back to the Bounty Booth on the eastern edge of those unclaimed lands. Normally he'd cash in. And normally he'd feel good about it. Another criminal down. A thousand more to go.

The whiskey was quenching his thirst, but not his conscience. He started eyeing up the bottles of liquid death inside the glass cabinets behind the bar. They had the kind of warning symbols on them that matched the star-shaped badge on his chest. Just one shot. That applied to the drink, and it applied to him.

Swill Roberts must've noticed, because he cocked his head and showed his yellow teeth in what he probably thought was a smile. He was waiting for Nox to ask for a glass. Boy was he tempted, but boy did he know it'd be a bad idea. He didn't have enough fingers to count the things the criminals would do to him if they found him dozing at the bar, and chances were he'd have a few digits less by the end of it. He couldn't afford the luxury of forgetting who he was or how he'd got there, no matter how much he wanted to forget. No, he'd have to stick with the good old mountain dew.

He tapped the rim of his glass, and the disappointed barman topped it up. Maybe he liked seeing what his poison could do to a man, but the Coilhunter was looking to be more than that. He needed to be a spectre, haunting every piece of scum that went to the Wild North looking to con and kill. He could only be in so many places, but the fear of him could be everywhere.

"What brings you this far west?" Swill Roberts asked. "Or should I say: who?"

Nox pulled the Wanted poster out of his pocket, along with the mechanical heart.

"Strawman Sanders," the barman mused. "Never heard of him."

"Well, you won't hear of him now."

"Is this … his?" Swill Roberts pointed at the clockwork organ.

"It's a little trophy from the Rust Valley."

"Is that so? Only other man I know who's got

anything from there is Batty Budford down in Edgetown. Says he wrestled a … a machine to get it. Mind, he's on the sundazzle by then."

"You'd wanna be if you wrestled with those things."

"So, you think they're real?"

"Oh, they're real all right. I seen 'em with my own two eyes."

"Thought they were just another scary story."

The Coilhunter smirked. "We're in the Wild North. All the scary stories are real."

Chapter Four

HELP

Swill Roberts was polishing up a glass, and Nox was polishing up his own, when the door burst open as if from a storm. There, panting and wheezing, was a girl of about fifteen or sixteen years, her blonde hair a mess, her eyes wild with terror.

"Help me!" she screamed, drawing the attention of anyone who wasn't giving their full attention to the table. "Please! They took my brother. I need help!"

Not a soul stirred. Swill Roberts kept on polishing, expressing a bit of sympathy at best. You see, sympathy was free. Sympathy didn't get you killed. Acting on it did.

The girl hobbled over to a table of men playing a drinking game, who didn't even give her that complimentary sympathy. She pawed at the arms and shoulders of one of them, who shrugged her off. She was lucky he didn't do worse.

"Please, sir," she begged. If they had to drink every time she pleaded, they'd have been out of alcohol real quick.

She stood in the centre of the room, arms out, looking as bedraggled as the worst of them, though maybe she had more reason to be. Her white shirt and black jeans were blood-splattered, though it looked like it was dried in well. "He's just a kid," she sobbed. "He has seizures. They'll … they'll kill him. They don't even know. He's been through so much. We've been … will no one help us?"

You could bet good money that she'd gone to the wrong place to look for help. She should've went far south, away from that God-forsaken place, and even then it'd have been a gamble.

"Will no one help?" she asked again. And, for quite a long moment, it looked like no one would.

Then Nox stood up. The gamble paid off.

He turned, adjusting his mask, which sent out a plume of smoke, like a signal fire. The girl froze, staring at him. He could see the fear in her eyes, could see her calculating if she should push her luck or run. Most people who pushed their luck in the Wild North ended up dead.

"Girl," the Coilhunter crooned. "Who took 'im?"

"I don't know," she said, reefing through her hair, which was part up and part down, and part in her hand. "Some gang."

That could've been anyone. There were so many gangs there, there weren't enough people for them to rob and murder. They often had to settle for taking out each other. Nox didn't mind that so much, except that innocent people often got caught in the crossfire. Innocent people like this girl and her brother.

Nox glanced at Swill Roberts and reached for his pocket, where the coils of past bounties clanged together like bones.

The barman held the glass up and nodded.

"Consider it a ... gesture of understandin'."

Nox knew what that meant. It meant turning a blind eye to whatever was happening there. *I scratch your back, and you don't stab mine.*

"Yeah, I don't think so," Nox said, flicking two full coils over to the barman. "I pay for what I owe. If you owe anything, you'll pay for it too." He left the clockwork heart as a tip.

He didn't wait for the barman's response. He wasn't a man of conversation. He was a man of action, and right now, he felt he had to act. It was like his conscience calling. You kill one, then you gotta save another.

He grabbed the girl by the arm and pulled her close. "I need more details. What were they wearin'? What'd they call each other? Where were they headin'?"

The girl racked her brain. She was in such a frenzy she probably couldn't think straight, couldn't remember the things that'd actually help her out. Maybe she didn't expect that someone'd help either.

Nox grabbed both of her wrists, knowing how much time was of the essence. "Think!"

"I ... they had a truck. I didn't really see 'em. It was night."

"Where were you when it happened?"

"About a mile east of here. We ... we had a campfire."

"Where'd they go?"

"North-east, I think. I ... I'm not sure."

"The truck. Did it have wheels or landship treads?"

"Treads, I think."

That wasn't much to go on, but it was enough for him. He had an eye for detail. He'd find those tracks if he was quick, if he got there before the shifting sands did.

"You wait here," Nox said, making for the door.

"No! He's my brother. I'm coming with you."

"You wait here or I won't go at all." Then Nox glanced around the room and saw one too many grinning faces. They were paying far more attention now that he was leaving. "On second thoughts, you better come with me."

They headed outside, where Nox clambered aboard his monowheel and ushered the girl into the box on the back. Normally you didn't want to sit in there. It was where he stored the bodies. He didn't tell her that.

"Can you save him?" she asked.

"Sure I can."

He didn't have the heart to tell her that the kid was probably already dead. But that didn't mean he'd stop trying. He knew all too well how bad the Wild North was, but he also knew it didn't have to stay like that. Bullet by bullet, he'd clean it out. It wasn't just a job. It was a mission. It was his life.

Chapter Five

TRACKS

Nox powered up the monowheel, which ran on a diesel engine, and rolled off. The giant treads that rotated around the outer wheel were perfect for the unsteady sands of the desert, but they left behind some pretty noticeable tracks. He was counting on the same for the truck.

The girl clung on behind him, hugging his oxygen tank. She should've been clinging to hope, but in Altadas hope had a way of slipping through your fingers like it was butter. Now, vengeance—that was something you could hold onto. Hell, if you let it, it'd hold onto you.

He heard her mutter something, but it was muffled by the wind. The sands were kicking up fierce now. It was like they knew he was on the hunt. They just couldn't let it be easy. No, in the Wild North, nothing came easy, except maybe death. You didn't just have to look over your shoulder. You had to look down to the earth beneath, and keep a wary eye.

He tilted the monowheel, making a sharp turn as he caught sight of the trail. He felt the girl's grasp tighten as she was thrown around in the back. She gave an involuntary grunt. Normally the passengers who sat back there didn't mind at all.

He leaned down on one side, scooping up a fistful of sand, just enough to see the half-buried track beneath. The whirling winds tried to blind him, so he kept the brim of his hat low. He knew they were scrubbing the path behind him too, burying his own trail. Maybe that way no one'd find him. Maybe one day they'd bury him too.

He pressed on through the haze and the grit, his own body shielding the girl from most of it. He wondered what her story was, and maybe if he was a different kind of guy, he might have asked. He tried not to know too much, tried not to get too close. He couldn't shield people from everything. He'd learned that all too well. Life had made a lesson out of him.

He halted at an abandoned campsite, where the girl hopped off and scoured the area. He stayed on his monowheel, feeling the humming engine beneath him, knowing they wouldn't find the boy there, knowing that with the sun bobbing low, they mightn't find him at all.

"His bag!" the girl cried. "This is his bag!" She held up a small threadbare satchel with one buckle broken. It'd seen better days, and maybe the boy hadn't seen any of them. A well-chewed pencil slipped out of the satchel, and the girl fumbled about for it in the sand.

"Come on," Nox said. "He's not here."

She hurried over, cradling the little leather bag. Nox didn't like the look of it. It reminded him too much of two little satchels just like it. He had them back at his hideout. For a while, he cradled them too. Then he locked them away, just like the memories.

They drove off again, against the flailing winds, which helped fill up that little satchel in the back. You never quite got used to the itch of the sand. You just learned to put up with it, learned to wear it like you wore your skin.

The tracks were faded, but the good thing about the shifting sands was that they kept on shifting. They might have buried things, but if you watched long enough, you'd see them uncover something else. Nox followed instinct more than anything, letting the periodic glimpse of the tracks confirm that he was heading in the right direction.

Then he spotted a light far ahead, so he killed his own. He parked the monowheel, hearing far-off voices as the engine's thrum died down. The wind whistled through it all, as if to say: nothing to see here.

"Is that them?" the girl whispered, crouching down beside the Coilhunter.

"Maybe." He ushered her back. "You stay here. And I mean it this time. No point rescuin' one of you if the other gets caught."

He stalked forward, feeling a different kind of itch in his fingers. Just like the mask now felt like it was a part of him, he could feel those pistols strapped to his thighs. This time the enemy was made of flesh and bone. This time he'd get to use them.

Chapter Six

THE NIGHT SLAVERS

There were three open-top trucks parked in a triangular formation, shielding a group of men in the middle from the lash of the wind.

"Quiet night," Oddman Rensley, a Rounder of the Night Slavers, said. "You sure we haven't been here before?"

"As sure as sunlight," Tinhead Tom, replied. He knocked on the metal plate welded into his skull, as if he thought it meant a promise. Nox knew well that the only thing about promises they knew was how to break them.

"As sure as dark, ya mean," Plump Podge corrected with a snicker. "We ain't no Sun Slavers."

They laughed their boisterous laughs, which the howling wind couldn't hide.

"We can't go back empty-handed," Oddman Rensley said. As a Rounder, he was used to rounding up as many as a dozen in a good night's work. It was his job to make sure the slaves kept coming in. Coilcountin' Lawson would get rid of them—preferably for a chunk of change. If not, well, someone else'd get rid of those.

"Well, it's Moonlit Jones' fault we've got this God-

34

damn route," Plump Podge said.

"He wouldn't have given us it if it weren't for yer yammerin'," Tinhead Tom replied. "It ain't yer fat belly that gets us in trouble. It's yer fat mouth."

The look on Plump Podge's face was priceless. Tom must've thought he'd struck a real nerve there, but Podge wasn't looking at him. He was looking up at the top of one of the trucks, where the Coilhunter was perched like a hawk.

"And what about yours?" Nox asked, before firing a single shot that gave Tinhead Tom another bit of metal in his head. "Well," the Coilhunter croaked. "I guess you won't be talkin' now."

Podge and Rensley scurried about inside the little prison they'd built for themselves, caught off guard, too clueless to reach for their guns. Not that it'd matter. The Coilhunter'd disarm them soon enough.

Podge struggled with the door of his truck. Just as he got it open and crawled inside, Nox swooped down and dragged him back out. The way that man squealed was a kind of justice in and of itself. Well, he'd never make another squeal just like him. Nox saw to that with a bullet between the eyes.

He heard the click of a hammer behind his head, but before Oddman Rensley could fire, he swung around, bashing the gun away with his own. The bullet pinged off one of the trucks and ricocheted off the others. Nox ducked just in time, but Rensley floundered as the little lead nugget pierced his shoulder.

Nox turned and leapt at him, pressing him against the hull. He felt Rensley already begin to slip. He was losing blood quick. It was a special kind of justice to die to your own bullet. In many ways, Nox felt that was how everyone went out in the end.

But not yet, Nox taught. *Not till you squeal for me too.*

Rensley groaned as the Coilhunter pressed his thumb into the wound. It wasn't just to hurt him. It was to stem the flow of blood. The slaver wouldn't look at him, kept bobbing his head away. It was no surprise that he didn't want to see the man who'd send him to his maker.

"You took a boy," Nox growled.

"We took a lot of boys."

"Last night. From a camp just south of here."

"Him? He was lucky we took him at all."

"What, didn't come willingly?" Nox grabbed the slaver's face real tight. "I know the feelin'."

"He's gone," Oddman Rensley said.

Nox felt his heart sink. He'd felt that before, and hoped to never feel it again. He hoped he could stop others from feeling it too.

"We already sold him," Oddman Rensley continued.

Nox perked up. That was good. That meant the kid was still alive. For now.

"That was a pretty quick sale," Nox observed. "Why, I might've patted ya on the back if I wasn't gonna break it."

Rensley gave a half-sigh, half-scream. "We sold him to a man who runs a grogshop not far from here. Goes by the name Swill Roberts. Needed a barboy to serve up all that rotgut he makes."

"See, now I know you're lyin'," Nox said. "And I like liars only a little more than I like slavers. Why, I've got a fist for either, and it looks like you might be gettin' both."

Nox raised his gloved fist, until it blotted out the remainder of the sun. Rensley shielded his face.

"All right, all right!" he cried. "He's probably still being … processed."

"What's that mean?"

"Evaluated. Y'know, to see how valuable they are."

Nox scoffed at the thought. In his eyes, this slaver wasn't worth much at all.

"Where d'ya do this processin'?" the Coilhunter asked.

"The Night Ranch."

"And where's that?"

"They'll kill me if I tell you."

Nox leant in close. "I'll kill you if you don't."

Chapter Seven

SLAVER NOX

The Coilhunter propped Oddman Rensley up in the passenger seat of the slaver's truck, before freeing the two men who were trapped in the back of another.

"Take these trucks," Nox told them, pointing to the two remaining vehicles. "It's the least the Night Slavers owe you."

They drove off, and Nox made Rensley direct him towards the Night Ranch. It didn't take much convincing. Men like him broke quicker than their slaves. But Rensley was starting to nod off from the blood loss, forcing Nox to shake him awake. He'd used Plump Podge's shirt as a bandage, but that was quickly turning crimson.

"You better not be lyin' to me," Nox said through his gritted teeth. The truck groaned as it crawled across the desert. Already he missed the speed of his monowheel.

He slapped Rensley in the face, something the man was getting used to.

"I'm not seeing it," Nox said.

"It's here … further up."

"How come I haven't cleaned this place out

before?"

"We're good."

"You're not that good," Nox crooned. "Why, you're not good at all."

Another slap. Rensley was starting to slump in his seat.

"Hang in there," the Coilhunter said. "We ain't finished yet."

Finally he saw the faint outline of the ranch in the distance. It looked like a sprawling estate, which surprised Nox quite a bit. He'd been back and forth across this area often. Yet, no matter how much you thought you knew the desert, it kept on surprising you. Nox tended to pick the same path most times— he couldn't call it a road, because there were few of those around—and he picked the fastest he could find. He could only imagine that the Night Slavers watched his routes and made their own outside of them.

He pulled up close to a sentry point, where there were quite a few armed guards. He felt like storming the place, like ramming through the barrier, but he knew the slavers would use the slaves as hostages. He had to play this one quietly.

A guard knocked on the door on his side and peered up. Nox smiled back down at him, but he had to do it with his eyes. He had his neckerchief tied across his face, obscuring the mask. It must've looked odd, but not as odd as what was beneath.

"What's the password?" the guard asked.

Nox whacked Rensley in the arm.

"Silver by … moonlight," Rensley grunted.

"What happened to him?" the guard asked.

"Same thing that happened to you," Nox said, dragging the man inside and snapping his neck. He didn't even have time to scream.

"Hell!" Rensley shouted.

"You're right," Nox said. "I guess it's a little different."

He forced the guard's body over the back of the truck. There was one big advantage this vehicle had over his monowheel. There was a lot more space for bad guys in the back.

Nox got out, yanking the barrier away. He got back in and drove on until he got to the next checkpoint, where there were several more guards. One of them tapped his rifle repeatedly against the side of the truck.

"How many?"

Nox presumed he meant: *How many slaves?*

"One."

"Just one?"

"It's a quiet night," Nox said. "But don't worry. We'll get more."

All three guards made their way around to the back.

Nox leant close to Rensley. "Whatever you do … stay still."

He unclipped a little capsule from his belt and lobbed it in the back.

The guards opened the door, their faces dropping when they saw the body inside. Those jaws dropped even more when the capsule cracked open and half a dozen tiny mechanical butterflies flooded out. The little creatures made straight for the guards, who were reaching for their weapons, or running, or calling out for help. They sprayed the moving figures with little puffs of noxious green gas, which knocked all of them out cold.

Rensley stayed as still as he could, afraid to even blink.

"Good," Nox said. "You're learning."

He got out, tapping a button on the panel on his wrist, which made all the little butterflies stop fluttering and collapse to the ground. He didn't bother scooping them up. He had many more toys up his sleeves.

He hauled the three guards into the back, piling them on top of each other. He was making quite a collection. He wondered if he could get a full set.

"You can blink now," Nox told Rensley when he got back in.

"You're … somethin' else."

"Yeah." Nox fired up the vehicle again.

"What … *makes* someone like you?"

"You do, Rensley. You do."

Chapter Eight

THE NIGHT RANCH

The Night Ranch was a sprawling settlement, with reinforced fences around its perimeter, which guarded against the sand storms. The slavers didn't just let the sand pile up there—they added some of their own, until it just looked like yet another dune from far away. With people like the Coilhunter on the loose, you couldn't just be quiet—you had to be *invisible*.

But Nox saw them now.

He was ushered on to a loading area filled with similar trucks. Some of them were just about to begin their rounds. Others had finished and were unloading the latest catch. The look of fear on those faces gave Nox a little more conviction—not that he needed any more.

"What now?" Oddman Rensley asked. He probably never felt odder, helping destroy the slaver business that'd been so good to him over the years. It wasn't doing him any good now. Nox didn't worry about Rensley tipping off the others. It was too late for all of them.

"This is where we part ways," Nox said. "I work better alone."

Rensley's face drooped a little more. "Are you ... going to kill me?"

Nox glanced at the wound. "No. I think *you* already did." He leant closer. "When you get to the other side, if you see anyone I didn't get a chance to kill ... well, tell 'em there's always a second chance to die. Doesn't matter if it's Heaven or Hell. Tell 'em I'm still comin' for 'em."

Nox hopped outside.

"Help me unload," he barked at one of the nearby guards.

He led the guard around to the back.

"Quite a catch, huh?" Nox said, before smashing the man's face against the door. If that guard ever ended up on a Wanted poster, Nox would recognise him from the busted nose.

Nox peered around the front again. "Could use a few more bodies back here."

Two more guards trotted over, helpful as ever. If only they could've hauled themselves inside. By the time Nox had cleared the area of guards, the truck was almost overflowing.

The Coilhunter followed the latest batch of slaves into a sorting shack, where they were counted and given a value. Nox would've almost said you couldn't put a price on a man, but then he'd made a living out of doing just that. If you asked him, the Bounty Booth was offering too much for some of them.

Nox slunk into the shadows near the door and watched the procession. It was amazing how much the slaves had already resigned themselves to their new fate. Not one of them showed defiance. They wanted to live, even if it wasn't really living. They marched when they were told to march. They halted when they were told to halt. Who knew what they would have done if they were told to die.

Coilcountin' Lawson was there, notepad in hand. He was a small man, dwarfed by many of the captives, and smaller still for what he did. His bald head was badly sunburnt, and his face wasn't much better. He had a horrid habit of licking his dirty fingers every time he turned a page, and boy did he turn a lot of pages. There were dozens of new slaves to process. He marked down their height, estimated their weight (to see how long you could go without feeding them), and listed one or two recommended "trades" for them—unpaid, of course. He seemed to delight in reading the poor men their fate, smiling sickly as he did. *Miner. Lumberjack. Millsman.* There wasn't a single woman in the crowd. Any of those that weren't taken to the slavers' personal dens were carted off immediately to the Black Silk Collective, a highly-secretive and decentralised organisation that kept the brothels of the Wild North well-stocked.

Nox continued to watch Lawson, imagining what he'd do to the man when he got his hands on him. For that kind of man, it wouldn't take much. It was almost a shame. But this wasn't about just making Nox feel better—though it did plenty of that—it was about doing some good.

"A poor catch tonight," Lawson said. What a name. He was the son of no law.

"Should still fetch plenty," Oil-hands Olly replied. Like most criminals in the Wild North, you could learn a lot about them by their names. He was a slick-fingered fellow, Lawson's best gunslinger, and probably the only reason that son of a gun wasn't already dead. It was also one reason why Nox felt he couldn't make a move yet. Oil-hands Olly would have those slaves gunned down in seconds.

"We still don't have enough for the Dew Distributors," Lawson complained. "That's two weeks in a row we've failed to fill their orders."

"Not many survive the waterworks," Olly said.

"That doesn't matter. We should have a constant influx."

"We're trying to be careful."

That was when Nox struck. "Not careful enough," he said, firing a bullet at the solitary light bulb casting a faint glow in the room. Everything went black. These slaves might have operated when the sun went down, but Nox was going to make them fear the night.

Chapter Nine

DRAWING IN DARKNESS

The Coilhunter and Oil-hands Olly fired in almost perfect unison, but Nox didn't fire a normal gun. He fired one of the grappling hooks from the spring-loaded device on his right arm, which hooked around one of the wooden pillars on the far end of the room. It acted like a tripwire to the fleeing slaves, who toppled to the ground, where they were safely out of the line of Olly's gunfire.

But Nox wasn't.

That quick-drawing conman almost didn't need daylight. His first bullet clipped the edge of the Coilhunter's oxygen tank as he dived. The next struck the wall just behind where he was last standing. He'd barely hit the floor before another one puckered the floorboards a little too close. It was almost as if Olly could see him, but Nox knew it wasn't that. It was the second sight you got with experience, with managing to fire a lot of guns, and avoid many more fired back at you. It was the kind of second sight the Coilhunter had as well.

Nox yanked a whole strip of butterfly capsules from his belt as he rolled, casting them into the centre of the room, where the slaves were still groaning.

Anyone who was wise enough to stay down was fine. Anyone who wasn't, well, the butterfly gas knocked them back to the floor just as quick. It was better than death. Death didn't wear off.

Nox snapped the grappling wire off with a flick of his dagger, then just as quickly exchanged it for a pistol. He fanned the hammer, unloading the barrel in an arc of fire at where Lawson and Olly had last been seen. He knew they probably both would've ducked for cover, but he just needed to suppress them long enough to find some better cover of his own.

The darkness helped and hindered in equal measure, which was more than could be said for the sun. In this case, the sightlessness just made their hearing more acute. That fast-fingered Olly could've heard Nox's boots a mile off. It was just as well, then, that Nox activated a noise-maker in the tip of the grappling hook across the room. The little device made a series of sounds just like Nox's fabled stompers.

He used the distraction to duck behind a stairway, allowing himself an inch of a smile as he heard Olly's bullets ping off the wall across the way. Some criminals said fighting Nox was like fighting ghosts. He seemed to come from everywhere. Most criminals who fought Nox never said anything at all.

Nox paid close attention to Olly's firing pattern. He seemed to fire in threes, and he'd draw a triangle with his shots if he didn't think you were running. Most people'd dodge out of one shot to be hit by the next. But it wasn't just the timing that Nox was paying attention to. The thing about gunfire is that it

47

made little flashes of light, and those flashes were like dynamite in the dark.

Nox aimed his gun and waited.

Bang.

They fired again in almost perfect unison. This time, Olly barely started his rounds at the decoy when he gave a grunt and fell flat on his face. Nox didn't bother firing in threes. One did the trick just fine.

He heard Lawson's petty little yelp, followed by the scurry of his feet. All Nox had to do was wait. The red-faced criminal ran straight into the swarm of butterflies, who were just looking for more movement to track. He didn't just yelp this time. He screamed as they latched onto his face, then slumped to the ground with a thud. There was no doubt he'd have bad dreams that night—if Nox'd let him have any at all.

Nox came out of his cover, just in time as a group of guards raced in from the back. They shone faint oil lanterns around the room, highlighting the dozens of bodies, which they thought were dead. Then they saw the Coilhunter's silhouette across the way, and they couldn't aim their weapons quick enough before he gunned them down.

Nox strolled over to where Coilcountin'—or make that Sheepcountin'—Lawson lay. The butterflies crowded around the Coilhunter, spraying their somniferous gas into his face. He could make useful toys, but he hadn't quite learned how to make loyalty yet. Not that it mattered. His mask filtered out the fumes.

He swatted the creatures away, then leant down

and yanked the little notepad out of Lawson's hand. He lit a match and flicked through the pages until he found what he was looking for: *Boy. Eight to ten years. Four foot, two inches. Estimated sixty pounds. Wild, dusty hair, pale complexion. Round face. Pouty demeanour. Curious eyes. Refused to give name, but carries a journal that says* Property of Luke Mayfield. *Ideal for the mines. Should fetch ten to fifteen coils easily. Some pay more for youth.* It listed two potential buyers, with a meeting arranged for the following morning. Nox was just in time.

He took Lawson's set of keys and headed through the rear door, down a long corridor of cells, where many more slaves were huddled. He couldn't let any of them out just yet. They'd draw even more attention than he did, and probably wouldn't get far before the rest of the slavers mowed them down in their trucks.

At the end of the corridor, he spotted a kid matching Lawson's meticulous description. The boy sat on his own in the corner, hugging his knees, with the sleeves of his plaid shirt rolled up past his elbows, and a small leather journal stuffed into his shirt pocket. His jeans were dusty, but they looked pretty new, new enough to know that his parents must've had money. You had to be careful how you dressed in the desert, because it wasn't just the Coilhunter who spotted those little details. The kid didn't even look up when Nox approached. He probably assumed that he was just like the rest of them, another gunman there to sell a child.

Nox tapped one of the keys off the bars. Everyone inside perked up. Maybe they thought it was feeding time. Maybe they thought they'd be seeing who their buyer was, and if they looked cold and cruel. The Coilhunter did.

"You," he croaked, pointing to the kid.

The boy looked up and trembled. He didn't brush away the sandy hair from his eyes. Maybe he didn't want to see.

"You got a sister?" Nox asked.

The kid seemed like he didn't know how to answer. Maybe he thought this masked menace meant something nefarious by it. Maybe he wondered if he should've lied. He didn't though.

"Y-y-yes, sir."

"Well, thank the high heavens you do … because she sent me to rescue ya."

The boy's face was like granite. He seemed too lost in his own thoughts to register what was happening. Nox sorted through the bunch of keys until he found the right one. He turned the lock, and the boy's face changed. It wasn't happiness though. It was surprise.

Nox didn't realise why until it was too late.

He heard the faint sound of a padded sole behind him, then the whoosh of air as something came down hard and heavy on his head. Then the sound of static. Then nothing at all.

Chapter Ten

SHADOW AND LIGHT

"Well, well, well."

As Nox came to, his head spinning and his vision blurred, the voice sounded like the Devil. Maybe it was.

"The Sandsweeper himself," the voice boomed. That was just one of the names they had for him. It seemed every gang Nox took on came up with something new.

Nox felt the ground beneath his knees, and rough fingers holding his arms behind his back. Someone had taken off his hat and was holding his head up by his hair. He could feel the air against the scarred patch above his left ear, where the hair refused to grow. They say the barren land got everywhere. Sometimes you became it too.

Then his eyes adjusted, and he saw who was talking. Moonlit Jones, a silver-haired man with bushy eyebrows and dark skin. No, not the Devil. Probably a little worse. Some thought the Coilhunter was like a ghost, but in all his long years policing the Wild North, he'd only ever heard of Jones. They said you could only see him in moonlight. But then they said stuff like that about the Coilhunter too.

"Sweepin' all the scum-filled sand out o' the Wild North," Jones said with a chuckle. "That's the thing about sand. The wind tends to blow it back up here. And the scum with it."

"Yeah," Nox said. "I can see that."

Then he saw something else. Behind where Moonlit Jones sat, someone stood in the darkness. You couldn't see their face. They seemed to be wearing a black mask. He had an idea who that was. People called him—or maybe it was her—the Shadow. That was it. No other names like Nox. He was fairly confident it was the Shadow that knocked him out.

He also noticed someone else to the side: Coilcountin' Lawson. He was a little bruised, but he had a smug smile on that fat lip of his. It was payback time. He'd even recovered his notepad so he could record all the gory details.

"There are a lotta people out there who'd pay good money for you," Jones said. "You've made a lotta enemies over the years. Why, you're more wanted than the rest of us."

The crowd erupted in laughter. Funny, that. Usually when they met the Coilhunter, no one laughed.

"The question is," Jones continued. "Are you worth more dead or alive?"

Nox could already feel the cold steel of the gun barrels against his neck and the back of his head. But he also knew the answer to Moonlit Jones' question. He'd already be dead otherwise. There was nothing like the prospects of more money—and the chance to make a few valuable friends—in the criminal underworld. It was something Nox could count on. Their greed. It'd be their downfall, even if he wasn't necessarily the one who'd see it.

They stared him down. If they couldn't kill him with guns, they'd try to kill his soul with their eyes. In their minds, they spat at him. He was a dog, a mangy runt that had caused a hell of a lot of trouble. There were mud stains on the floor. Soon, there'd be blood stains too.

But while they were staring and laughing, and talking amongst themselves about how the fabled Coilhunter didn't look so threatening after all, Nox adjusted his arms behind his back, tapping a few buttons on his wristpad. No one saw him do it. The same speed he used to draw a gun helped him with everything.

But Nox didn't have the time or opportunity to be smug. He knew they didn't just want to kill him. They wanted to break him, and they'd use anyone they thought he was close to.

So they used the boy.

It was a sorry sight to see four grown men drag a child into the room. That kid didn't come willingly. He struggled against their massive hands, but he struggled in vain. Nox was surprised that they hadn't already killed him. A slave like that was too much trouble. But then there were some mines that only children could fit into. That made them valuable. Maybe they thought that they could break the boy too.

"So, who's this, huh?" Jones asked, pointing to the kid. "I thought your boy was dead."

Nox bit his lip. He felt his chest heaving. He had to take a few slow, deep breaths, the kind that brought more of that mixture of chemicals into his lungs. He had to bury that part of him that still hurt, the part that was still on fire. He had to bury it like he swore he'd bury Moonlit Jones.

"Not as dead as you're gonna be," he croaked.

Jones scoffed. "You're in no position to be brave, Nox. You're in the Valley of Darkness now."

Nox didn't say a word. He waited, counting the seconds in his mind. Sometimes you counted bullets and sometimes you counted time. Either one could kill you.

"Who's the kid?" Jones asked again, staring at the boy. He let his hand dangle over the armrest of his chair, that hand with all its many gem-encrusted bands. Maybe you didn't really see Moonlit Jones at all. Maybe in moonlight you'd only see his rings.

"He's nobody," Nox said, trying not to even glance at the kid, trying to forget the name he'd read in Lawson's notebook. *Property of Luke Mayfield.* He couldn't help but wonder if the boy would be branded soon: *Property of Moonlit Jones.*

"Didn't seem like nobody when you were tryin' to bust 'im out."

"Just a kid," Nox insisted. "Don't even know his name."

Nox wasn't entirely lying. That journal could've belonged to anyone. The thing about the Wild North was that your property often didn't remain yours for long. So, not quite a lie and not quite the truth. And it looked like Jones realised it too, realised that Nox's connection to this kid was passing. That crime boss furrowed his brow in confusion. No doubt he was thinking: *Then why risk your life for him?*

"You don't get it," the Coilhunter explained, buying himself the time he needed. "I'm not like you, Jones. I care what happens to good people. I care what happens to innocent people."

He glanced at the boy, and the child looked as surprised as Jones was. In the Wild North, a lot of children had to grow up feeling like no one cared about them. For many, it wasn't even just a feeling. If you didn't grow up feeling like that, then you were probably dead.

"But here's the thing," Nox continued, settling his eyes like crosshairs on Moonlit Jones. "I don't care what happens to you."

Then, like clockwork, the cavalry arrived. The monowheel crashed through the wooden wall, sending splinters in all directions like missiles. It had no driver, though the girl was still sitting in the box at the back, holding on for dear life. She had to hold on tight.

People ran and jumped out of the way, and others reached for their guns.

"Duck!" one of the guards shouted.

Many of the people covered their heads with their hands, dropping to the floor. They expected a hail of bullets. After all, that's how they would've done it.

But they weren't Nox.

Most of them hadn't noticed a little hatch open in the side of the monowheel. They hadn't spotted the little toy duck that waddled down a small ramp. When they did, their jaws dropped, their eyes widened, and they tried to run.

The duck turned its head. Its little beady eyes surveyed the room.

Quack.

The explosion made dynamite seem like a faint clap in comparison. But this wasn't fire and gunpowder. This was what the Night Slavers hated the most. This was light.

Chapter Eleven

BLINDSIDED

Everyone was seeing white. Not just the normal colour either. A blinding, burning white, a bit like staring straight up at the sun. Nox didn't know how much long-term damage his device did to people's retinas, but he knew the short-term effects real well. It worked.

People dropped their weapons and crawled across the floor. Some clawed at their eyeballs, screaming and rolling about. Others knocked themselves out by running into walls or doors. It was chaos. It was just how Nox needed it to be.

He used his wristpad to send the monowheel back outside, and the girl with it. Then he struck the guard to his right, and tried the same to the left, but that one was already fleeing. They'd taken his guns, but he heard some of them drop their own. He felt along the ground, feeling other hands, then a face here and there, and someone's empty shoe. It was funny what people abandoned, like their conscience.

He was waiting for the adjustment, for the light to dim just a little, for when he'd start seeing pale glimmers of silhouettes. But it was taking a long time. He just had to hope that everyone else was as blind as he was.

Then the tip of his finger touched something metal, moving the object a little across the floor. The sound stood out more now, and he heard someone else crawling towards it too. He threw himself forward. Both his hand and someone else's grabbed the gun.

Nox swiped with his other hand, but struck thin air. Then he felt a fist against his forearm. Then he heard a cry as the man punched the ground. Nox yanked the gun from his grasp and pushed the barrel against the man's torso, to make sure he wasn't killing anyone else. He fired, and the shot sounded like thunder to everyone's sensitive ears.

There were several answering shots. It was largely panic. Nox heard them ping off the walls in all directions. No one cared who they hit, so long as it wasn't them. That made it way more dangerous for the rest of them.

Nox pulled his guitar out and held it before him as he crawled along. It was just as well he did, because he heard one shot strike the reinforced metal frame.

He heard the boy cry out across the room. He scrambled over, ducking behind the guitar, trying not to strike the strings. Any time it hit the floor, the vibration sent out a little tune. It was better than the music of gunfire.

Nox patted the ground as he went, grabbing someone's ankle. He didn't know whose it was, but by the size he could guess it was an adult, and by the hairs he could guess it was a man's. He reached out until he felt a coat tail, then aimed his gun and fired.

It could've been anyone, but where Nox was, the odds were that it was a criminal.

He scrambled along further, towards the whimpers of the child. He could hear the flurry of fabric, so he knew there was a struggle. That kid had some fight in him. The question was: how long would he have some life in him too?

Nox tapped at his wristpad, firing up the monowheel again. He heard the girl shriek as it jolted forward, and then heard another cry from someone else as the wheel rolled over their arm. He halted the vehicle. He couldn't operate like this. The criminals mightn't have cared who died, but he did. If he got his way, it'd only be them.

He grabbed the boy's arm, pulling him behind the guitar. Bullets stuttered off the other side, pinging off in all directions, taking down more shapeless figures. Nox could hear the boy's heavy pants. They were lucky there was gunfire or everyone else would've heard them too.

"Find your sister," the Coilhunter told the child, giving him the guitar for cover. There wasn't room enough behind it for the both of them. If the kid had been a little bit older, he might've given him a gun as well. He thought there might still be time for that.

The boy was clearly dazed. Nox didn't need his sight to know that. The kid didn't murmur a response, didn't make any of the usual protests. He just clutched that guitar tightly, letting the cuff of his shirt pluck the strings. It almost played the Coilhunter's usual tune, that little lullaby Nox used before he put the criminals to sleep.

"Stay down," Nox told the boy, pushing him on towards where he could hear the thrum of the monowheel's engine, to where he could get the waft of the diesel fumes. He just hoped the kid's sister would stay there too.

The spotless white dimmed a little, enough for him to see the beginnings of shapes, dark blotches that might have been people. Some said it was in this state that you could see the real person, if they were man or monster. The Resistance had tried to rope him into their war against the Iron Empire for years, hoping he'd offer up his toys—hoping he'd help reveal just how demonic their enemy really was. But the real monsters operated up here in the Wild North, in the lands untouched by the war, in the wilds untouched by the law—except for the Coilhunter.

The silhouettes were something frightening. Nox now knew what the criminals felt when their vision adjusted and they saw him towering over them, the black mark of justice in their strained vision. He'd let a few of them go, as a warning to the others. He knew he'd be back for them in their dreams.

But what Nox feared more than anything was letting the criminals and conmen win. Nothing else mattered. So, he stood up, and glanced around, searching for the shapes he knew quite well, the shapes of men in cowboy hats that far too often made their way onto Wanted posters. Nox's sight started to return to normal, and all those dark shapes became more concrete. They were people all right, and most of them were dead. Except for one.

Nox strolled over to Coilcountin' Lawson, who

was pressing his hands against his wounded knee. It wasn't Nox's bullet that did that, but he'd do the rest. Lawson looked up at him with teary eyes and a trembling lip. He might've pleaded for his life if he thought it'd do him any good.

"Where are the others?" Nox asked, pointing his pistol at him.

"They're g-g-gone."

"I know they're gone. I can see that … now. But where? Where do the Night Slavers go when somethin' like this happens?"

Lawson furrowed his brow. "Somethin' like this? Nothin' like *this* happens!"

"Well, you should've known. You should've been expectin' me."

"They'll kill you for this!" Lawson growled. "You can count on it!"

"Well, you're good at countin', aren't ya? So, tell me," Nox said, pulling the hammer back on his pistol. "How many more bullets have I got in this gun?"

Lawson took a breath, as if to speak. It was his last. The little clap of thunder from Nox's gun masked the criminal's sigh.

"None now," Nox said, flicking open the empty barrel.

He took some new bullets from a pouch on his belt and loaded it up. The Night Slavers might have disappeared into their favoured darkness, but a new day would dawn soon enough, and that'd mean plenty more criminals waking up from their far too comfortable beds. Nox'd find them new ones, six feet down in the sand below.

Chapter Twelve

FREE

They say there's no rest for the wicked, but there didn't seem to be any for the good either. When Nox found the kids outside, the girl was leaning over the boy on the ground. The boy was convulsing, his arms flaying about in the sand.

Nox raced over, kneeling down beside them.

"What happened?"

"It's his seizures," the girl said. "He has them from time to time."

"There any medicine?"

The girl shook her head. "I don't know. We don't have any."

"What do you normally do?"

She sighed and held the boy's hand tighter. "Just wait it out."

Nox looked at the boy. His body shook violently, his eyes rolling in all directions, his tongue lolling in his mouth. He wanted to help the poor kid, but for once he felt like he didn't know how. He had no gadgets or weapons for something like this.

"Maybe it's the stress," Nox suggested, placing his hand on the boy's shuddering shoulder. "Probably all that gunfire."

"Or your bomb," the girl said curtly. She glanced suspiciously at the duck, which stood guard beside the monowheel.

"It ain't a bomb."

"It sure seemed like one."

"If it was a bomb, we'd all be dead."

"You almost killed us all anyway."

"I *saved* you," Nox replied. "I saved your brother."

The girl was about to respond when the boy's tremors suddenly subsided.

"Ugh," the boy said.

"You're back," his sister replied, her eyes tearing up.

"Where'd I go?"

She pursed her lips. "It happened again."

"Is it gettin' worse?"

She didn't respond.

The boy turned his head towards Nox, his eyes wide. That was the usual look most gave him.

"Who're you?" the boy asked.

"Just a drifter."

"Are you one of … *them*?" The child's eyes indicated the building they'd just come out of.

"No."

"He saved you," his sister said, handing him back his satchel.

The boy struggled to sit up, resting his elbows on the ground. He looked around, giving a double take when he saw the little toy duck staring at him.

"Mr. Quacky!" he cried, smiling. He turned back to Nox. "That must make you, um, Mr. Wacky." He grinned, and his sister slapped him on the arm. "But he is," the boy insisted.

Nox grumbled and stood up. "Right, well … I guess this is where we part ways."

The girl nodded solemnly. She knew better than to hope for more. She'd already gotten more than she expected. She was old enough to know that the desert didn't owe you a thing—though it'd give you a six-foot hole if you waited long enough.

"Where'll we go?" the boy asked, pushing himself up.

"Go find your family, boy."

The boy's eyes lit up with a kind of terror Nox did not expect. He gave a slight shake of his head, as if he didn't want the Coilhunter saying that around his sister.

"We're trying to find 'em," the girl said. "That's why we came out here."

"Out here?" Nox asked. "There ain't nothin' out here."

"They came this way."

"They're dead," the boy said, frowning.

"They're not dead," his sister replied. "We don't know that. They can't be. It hasn't been long enough. We'll find 'em, Luke."

Luke. So the name was right. That journal wasn't stolen. Nox almost wished it was. That way, he still wouldn't know the kid's name. It'd be easier then, easier to move on, to not get attached. He couldn't help but see a row of graves in his mind, getting steadily smaller, each of them etched with a name he knew too well.

The boy didn't seem convinced by his sister's

comments. He looked at Nox with almost pleading eyes, those eyes that the Coilhunter now associated with a name. Luke's breathing started to get heavy again. Nox was a little concerned he might have another seizure.

"How long's it been?" Nox asked.

"Two months," the girl replied.

Luke pouted. "It's three. It might even be four!"

"It's not!"

Nox knew it didn't matter. Two months was long enough. If their parents were missing that long, chances were they were dead. Often it only took a day. Sometimes, just an hour.

"Where'd you last see 'em?" Nox asked.

"At our home," the girl said.

"Where's that?"

"Close to Dawn's Watch."

"Why, that's miles from here."

"I know."

"Why don't you go back? Wait for 'em there."

"We can't, it's—"

"It's gone," Luke said. "Raiders burned it down."

"Oh."

"So we started lookin' for our parents," the girl explained.

"*She* did." The boy folded his arms. "I didn't want to."

"Why not?" Nox asked.

"'Cause I know they're gone too."

"You don't know that!" the girl yelled, bashing her fist against the sand in frustration.

"They went into the Rust Valley," Luke said, as if

that was all he needed to say. It was.

Nox let out an involuntary sigh, which sent a plume of smoke out of his mask. The girl didn't want to believe it, but if their parents wandered into that scrapyard dungeon, there was no chance they'd be coming out alive.

Chapter Thirteen

WITHOUT A HOME

The Coilhunter sent the other former slaves on their way, back to their homes, or to where they might find new ones. There was no end of free land in the Wild North, but not much of it was fertile. You had to make do with what you got, and pay a levy to the Dew Distributors for a shipment of water to keep you going. Once you stopped paying, the shipments stopped—and so did you.

But Nox found it difficult to send these children away. They weren't the first kids to lose their parents and home, and wouldn't be the last. Sometimes it was the other way around, and the parents wandered alone. Nox could make many people follow his rules, but Death was entirely outside of the law.

He heard the kids arguing over where they'd go, and again the boy seemed on the verge of one of his attacks. It was a sorry sight to see, not just because of the strain it must've caused the child, but because if you didn't get used to dealing with the stresses of the Wild North, you tended not to live long at all.

"Please, Laura," the boy said, pawing at her arm.

Laura. There was the second name. Nox couldn't escape it now, couldn't keep them in his mental vault of anonymous people. Most of the names he knew were the ones from posters, those names that had a lot of character to them, and a lot of crime. Laura and Luke just didn't fit in.

Laura tried not to look at her brother, staring out into the distance, at the vague silhouette of the Rust Valley. "They're out there," she said. "I know it."

Luke's eyes watered up. It seemed like they'd had this argument many times before, and perhaps on every occasion it ended with those same words. Then they'd walked farther west, braving the wilds, seeking what might never be found—and what might kill them.

Luke caught sight of Nox and quickly dried his eyes.

"Everything okay?" the Coilhunter asked.

"Yeah," Laura said. She seemed unused to someone asking a question like that without an ulterior motive.

Luke said everything wasn't okay, but he said it with his eyes.

"You're not going that way, are you?" Nox asked, gesturing to the scrapyard desert.

"We are," Laura stated. She tied up the rest of her hair, as if she'd let nothing get in her way.

"You know even I wouldn't go there."

"We're not you."

"No." No, they weren't. They were two kids, without armour, and without guns. The Clockwork Commune would make short work of them. And no one'd even know. Except Nox.

"It's been a big night," Nox said. "Let's get some

rest first."

If it wasn't for her fatigue, Laura might've protested the notion. Yet she knew they'd fare better after some sleep and food, and would travel farther under the spotlight of the sun. The desert air was growing quickly chill. Luke shivered from more than just the cold.

Nox set up a camp, using some of the wooden walls of the Night Ranch to light a fire. At least that prison had some use now.

Luke sat with his back against the monowheel, doodling in his journal. He didn't seem quite as agitated now. Nox had bought them another night. Maybe he didn't think about the day.

"How old are you, boy?" Nox asked.

Luke looked up from his journal, a little surprised. "I'll be ten in seven months."

"So, you're nine."

The boy scowled. "Yeah."

"He's been countin' down the days to ten since we started walkin'," Laura said.

"What's so good about bein' ten?" Nox asked.

Luke took a deep breath. "That's when I'll be a man."

"Oh?"

"Yeah. That's what papa said, anyhow." He seemed to almost regret mentioning his father, and stuck his pencil into his mouth to shut himself up. He looked back and forth between Laura and Nox. "That's when you get to make your own rules."

Nox smirked, but the boy didn't see it. "Is that so?"

"Uh-huh. Don't you?"

"I don't make the rules. I just enforce them."

The boy looked at Nox's belt, where the pistols gleamed in the firelight. This child was almost an open book. You could tell what he was thinking by where his wandering eyes went. It was a rare thing in the Wild North, because it was the kind of thing that got you killed. You had to learn to lie quick. Didn't matter if you were good or bad. You lied or you were dead.

"Do you like killin' people?" Luke asked eventually.

"I don't hate it."

"But d'you like it?" The boy kicked at a rock disinterestedly.

"No," the Coilhunter said.

"Then why d'you do it?"

"Someone's gotta clean up this place."

"Does it have to be you?"

"You ask a lotta questions, boy."

Luke shrugged. "Nothin' else to do."

The Coilhunter almost smiled. "Ever tried killin' people? Certainly passes the time."

The boy forced a smile.

"He's good at drawin'," Laura said. "Show 'im your drawin's."

Luke blushed. "I'm not that good."

"Well, that'll make two of us then," Nox replied.

He moved over next to the kid, and was very surprised by the quality of the drawings. These weren't just the doodles of a child. These were the first intimations of an artist. In another time, he might've made good money on that.

"Wow," Nox said.

"I told you they weren't very good."

"No. They're somethin' else. Why, I ain't even seen this good on Wanted posters."

"Really?"

"Yeah."

"Told ya," Laura said. "He keeps sayin' he's no good, and I keep tellin' 'im he's talkin' nonsense."

"You should listen to your sister," Nox said.

The boy's worried eyes returned.

Except when she's tellin' you to go into the Rust Valley, Nox thought. He decided it better not to say it, to let the night pass without mention of that tricky subject. Maybe by day, they'd forget all about it, like you forget your dreams.

"He could be one of those famous people," Laura said proudly. "Mama always said he could. Didn't mama always say it, Luke?"

Luke nodded meekly.

"You're lucky you're up here," Nox said, which was about the only time he ever said that about the Wild North. "Folks say you ain't allowed to draw stuff down south."

"Unless it's of the Iron Emperor," Laura added.

And folks didn't just say it. They died for it. The Regime's culture ban spanned most of Altadas, everywhere bar the rule-less waste of the Wild North. Even Resistance territory had little artwork, for fear that a battle would put it into enemy hands, and from there into the fire. Most of the great paintings of old were hidden away, locked in so-called "culture caches" at the bottom of the sea, or far up in the sky. One day, they might be seen again. Until then, any artist who wanted to live came up north. It wasn't just the criminals who fled from the law.

"I did a drawin' of him too," Luke said, flicking through his journal until he showed an image of a demonic being.

"Is that the Iron Emperor?"

"They say he's a demon."

"They do say that."

"I think he probably looks like this."

Nox knew better. The Bounty Booth was operated by the Regime, their small attempt to gain some input into the burgeoning bounty hunter business, and direct some of those bounties against Resistance targets. Nox had met plenty of Regime men—and they were men. But then, perhaps men and demons weren't so different after all.

"You gotta draw somethin' for me some time," Nox said. "The only pictures I've got are these Wanted posters, and I can't say I want one of them on my wall."

The boy tapped his pencil against his head, then chewed on the end again. It was an awful bad habit that reminded Nox too much of Strawman Sanders and his piece of straw. He didn't like the parallel, nor the possibility that the boy might be going to that same place where Sanders died.

"You shouldn't chew on that."

"Why not?"

"It'll poison you."

The boy looked at the pencil, then stuck it back in his mouth. "It hasn't yet."

"How do you know?"

The kid shrugged.

"Could explain those seizures of yours."

The boy looked away, embarrassed. Yet something in the look told Nox a little more. It was the same kind of look he'd seen many conmen give when he challenged them. It was the look of a liar.

Chapter Fourteen

WHY THE RUST VALLEY
BECKONED

The night lengthened, and Luke fell fast asleep, clutching his satchel. You'd think he'd have trouble sleeping out there, but it seemed he'd gotten used to it. If nothing else, exhaustion helped. Nox was still up, brooding, and he wasn't the only one. Laura couldn't sleep either. She stared at the fire.

"Worried?" Nox asked, sitting down beside her. He didn't look at the flames. He had them etched into his memory—and etched into his skin.

"Been worried since this all started."

"You know you could make it worse."

"I know," she said, "but I can also make it better."

Rarely did things work out that way in the Wild North, but that didn't stop Nox from trying. He knew he'd be a hypocrite to tell her to stop. The difference was, he'd already gotten used to how things worked in the desert. He knew when to fight and when to hide. He knew when to accept that he couldn't change something, and focus on what he really could.

Laura glanced at him. "Maybe you … can help us?"

"I thought I already did."

"I mean—"

"I know what you meant."

They were both silent for a moment, casting more stares into the flames. Nox hated those momentary glances. Even when he closed his eyes, the flames burrowed through his eyelids. He had to take a deep breath and let the black smoke from his mask dull the embers. He had to tell himself that it was all over, that he wasn't at that burning house, that he wasn't trying to save his family. It was over. They were dead. He'd had his vengeance, though it had taken far too long to get it. And it only helped a little. Here he was, still out in the desert, still seeing the flames, still looking for criminals, as if all of them were to blame.

"There's certain lands ya just don't walk," Nox said in time. "Like the lands of death, and that's what that scrapyard valley is. It ain't our territory. We're out here on the frontiers, but that land there, girl, is the frontier of life. D'ya understand?"

She nodded solemnly. He knew that nod. He'd made it himself far too many times. It was knowing that the path ahead was difficult—maybe even doomed—but walking it anyway. You could understand something plain and clear, but it didn't mean you had to do what it said.

"It's just," the girl began, catching her breath. "I don't think I can do this."

"Do what?" He knew she didn't mean venturing into the Rust Valley. She had the gumption for that all right, even if the Coilhunter didn't.

"Be what mama was."

"What was she?"

"No. I mean, to Luke."

"Oh." He paused. "You really care about him, huh?"

"Yeah. I'm all he's got left."

"So why d'ya wanna go and risk that?"

"'Cause we can get it all back. We can—"

"You can't go back to the way things were." Nox knew he was saying it to himself as much as her. You trudged on, step by step, until the desert took you too.

"But we have a shot."

"A shot in the dark. And you ain't no gunslinger."

That same solemn nod. "But you are."

"You ain't the first to try to get me to fight their war," Nox said. "And that's what it'd be, girl. If we enter Clockwork Commune territory, it'll be all guns blazin', and blazin' on all sides. Now, I ain't no army, and you ain't no soldier. And you can sure as hell bet that those constructs won't have no value in your brother's drawings. So why start a war you know you can't win?"

She didn't respond. The silence just allowed the echoes of the question to play out in Nox's mind, reminding him of his own unwinnable war against the never-ending tide of conmen and criminals. He was trying to clean up these parts, but every time he rubbed away a stain, he found another layer of dirt beneath. So, you could give up—or you could keep on scrubbing.

"Why'd they go in there anyhow?" Nox asked. He was curious, but he also just wanted to break the silence. The silence was like the flames, another reminder that they were gone.

"They're scientists."

Mad scientists, Nox thought. They'd have to be mad to do their research in there.

"Mama said she had a breakthrough."

Or a breakdown, Nox thought.

"She was researchin' how to make unlimited energy or somethin'."

"Perpetual motion?" Nox asked. "That old chestnut?"

"Somethin' like that. She said the constructs had the key."

The last Nox'd heard, those constructs relied on each other to keep themselves powered up. That was why they formed a commune, and why they kept to themselves. People would send their old vehicles in there to keep the peace, kind of like a sacrificial offering. The constructs used them to replace the broken bits of themselves. That way they could live forever. Perpetual motion of a different kind.

"And what about your old man?"

"Papa just does what mama tells him to do."

Nox smirked. "Guess he ain't ten yet, huh?"

"He always tells us 'don't do this', and then he does it himself."

"The way of the world, girl."

"He told us never to put ourselves in dangerous situations."

"He mightn't have listened to himself, but maybe you should."

She rolled her eyes. "You're soundin' like my brother. We'd already be in the Rust Valley if it wasn't for his seizures slowin' us down. I think they're gettin' worse."

"How long's he had 'em?"

"About the time our parents left."

About the time, Nox thought.

"I'm worried about him," Laura said. "I don't think I can help him. But maybe mama can."

If mama's still alive, Nox thought. You see, ghosts couldn't help with much.

Chapter Fifteen

DECISIONS

N ox couldn't force Laura to abandon her quest, and he couldn't blame her either. If it were him, he'd probably have done the same. He told himself that in the grand scheme of things, none of this mattered. Those kids'd be just another faceless figure on the Wild North's death list. He couldn't change peoples' minds, and he couldn't save everyone.

But the problem with reason and logic was that it had little effect on the heart. He felt compelled to help them, just as he felt compelled to clean up the region. He knew, deep down, that a lot of it had to do with those little gravestones he visited once a week in the more fertile lands far west, and his desire not to see two more stone slabs added to the desert's graveyard.

"Today's the day," Laura said. "We're very close."

Luke packed his things silently—resignedly. Every so often Nox caught a glance from the boy, as if he was checking in to see if maybe the Coilhunter would stop them, hoping he might.

They're not my kids, Nox thought to himself. It was supposed to help, make him feel like he could shirk some of the blame, but then so many of the people he saved were not his people—and he felt responsible for them all the same. This was what happened when you appointed yourself sheriff of the wastes. You couldn't hand in your badge whenever you felt like it. The desert was your domain, maybe even the scrapyard parts of it.

"Have you thought about supplies?" Nox asked.

Laura looked up. "Supplies?"

"For where you're goin."

"We've got our supplies."

Nox looked at their meagre belongings. She had a small backpack, from which hung a few pots and utensils, just enough for a quick campfire meal. Even Nox ate better than that, though he rarely ate in front of other people. He rarely did anything in front of other people, apart from cocking a gun.

"What about weapons?"

"We don't have any," Luke said.

"Mama said the constructs aren't aggressive if you're not."

Tell that to Strawman Sanders, Nox thought.

"Plus," Luke said solemnly, before pointing at his sister. "She used 'em all. Papa's rifle too."

"Still," Nox said. "Maybe you should come with me to get better supplies."

Luke perked up, but Laura saw through the Coilhunter's ruse.

"We're fine as we are."

Laura trotted westward, waiting for no one. Luke slumped his shoulders again and sauntered after her, kicking the sand as he went. The sun was unusually kind that morning, holding back its typical burn, as if even it was looking down with a sympathetic eye.

Then suddenly Luke started to twitch, one arm spasming erratically.

"Oh no," he chirped. He said it so quietly, Laura shouldn't have been able to hear, but she halted and looked back. Nox caught their exchange, the look of embarrassment and shame on the boy's face, the look of worry and exasperation on the girl's. It seemed that both of them said silently: *Not again.*

By the time Nox caught up, Luke was shaking violently and starting to panic. He took sharp, shallow breaths, and his face was flushed. It seemed like he was trying to fight through, to take another step forward, but his body was fighting back.

Laura raced back just in time to catch her brother as he fell. His arms flailed about madly, his legs kicking against the air. He looked in every direction, avoiding eye contact, until he caught the Coilhunter's gaze and seemed to grow afraid.

"It's okay," Nox said, attempting to be comforting, but the mask muffled his voice, and the grit in his throat made it come out coarse. He knew it was not okay, but not for the reason Laura thought.

It passed just as quickly as it came, quicker than most times, from the surprise and relief on Laura's face. But the boy was exhausted, barely able to sit, let alone walk to the Rust Valley.

"I'm sorry," he murmured, again avoiding eye contact with his sister.

She bit her lip. She should've said it was fine, but it wasn't. He was holding her back, slowing her down. She clearly didn't want to say it, and didn't want to feel it either. How many times was this now? How many days had his seizures delayed their journey?

"We can wait a little longer," Nox suggested. "I'll stay a little longer."

Laura nodded, then stood up. She looked around, grasping the back of her neck, where her hair was matted with sweat. She stared at the dark mountain of metal in the distance. She took long, deep breaths for Luke's short, shallow ones.

"I'll … I'll just scout ahead a bit," she said, almost choking on the words.

Luke looked up, but only saw the back of her. "But come back," he said.

Laura walked off slowly. "Yeah." She dropped her bag off as she went, her silent promise that she'd return.

Then it was just the boy and Nox. The kid slouched down, hanging his head.

"Well, now," Nox said. "Isn't this a pickle?"

Luke glanced up at him, but found it hard to keep his gaze. "What?"

"How often does this happen? The seizures."

"I … I don't know."

"You're pretty good at it," Nox said.

The boy's eyes widened.

"And I know why you do it."

Luke's eyes widened further.

"But you shouldn't lie to your sister," Nox added.

"I … I … uh—"

"It's okay. I won't tell her. But you should."

Luke hid his head away again. "I only did it to stop her going west."

"I know."

"I didn't think she'd keep tryin'."

"I know."

"Or that I'd have to keep doin' it."

"She's worried about you. And she'll find out eventually. What'll you do then?"

The boy shrugged. "I hadn't thought that far ahead."

"She might be the only family you've got left."

"But that's why I don't want us to go in there!"

"I know."

"Can't you do somethin'?"

"I'm not sure I can. Why, I can't exactly take you hostage."

"Can't you?"

"Haven't you had enough of slavers?"

Luke shrugged again. He placed his chin on his knee and sighed audibly.

"I didn't mean to lie to her," he said, pouting. He looked at Nox. "Honest."

"Well, there's what you mean, and there's what you do."

"I guess."

"I don't guess," Nox said. "I know."

Chapter Sixteen

GOOD OLD HONESTY

The day broadened, but the sun kept its uncharacteristic restraint, saving its scalding rays for someone else. When Laura returned, a little refreshed, Luke almost seemed like he'd have another seizure. But this time he shook a little because he was nervous, because he was afraid.

"Are you okay?" Laura asked, fresh worry filling her face.

"Yeah. It's just ..." The boy looked at Nox, then looked away to the sightless sand.

"It's just what?"

"I need to … I need to tell you somethin'."

"Okay."

"Will you promise you won't be mad?"

Laura stared at him for a moment. "I promise."

"Pinky swear?"

"Just tell me, Luke."

"I might've been … I might've been ..."

"You might've been what?"

Luke grasped his hair, almost pulling it from the roots. "Lyin'," he murmured. He flinched, as if he expected a smack.

Laura took a slight step back. "What were you

lyin' about?"

"Please don't make me say it."

"Say it, Luke. What were you lyin' about?"

"I didn't want to," he said. "I didn't mean to."

"*Luke.*"

"Don't be angry with me, sis," he pleaded. "Please."

"Luke!"

"The seizures," he croaked.

Laura shook her head. Her brow furrowed. "I don't understand."

A tear rolled down Luke's cheek. "I was … I was fakin' it." He bit his lip, but still it trembled.

Laura took another step back, a bigger one this time. "No."

"I didn't want you to go," Luke cried.

"No," Laura said again, shaking her head in large, slow motions.

"I didn't mean for it to get outta hand."

Another step back. "No."

Luke stepped forward. "Please, sis. I wasn't thinkin'. I just … please, sis."

It was painful for Nox to watch, but he knew that lies like this didn't do any good. In the Wild North, they were as plentiful as the sand itself. You couldn't take a step without bumping into one.

"All this time," Laura said, running her fingers through her hair. She turned away, glancing in all directions, except back at her brother. She stopped to look at the Rust Valley in the distance, then turned back to Luke. "We coulda been there!" she shouted. "We coulda been there already!"

"I know," Luke said, trotting forward. "I didn't

want us to go."

"You coulda just said that, Luke." She backed away again.

"I *did* say it. You didn't listen."

"You might've killed them, Luke."

He halted, his breath jittering. "Don't say that."

"All this time you were lyin', stoppin' us from goin'."

"I didn't mean to do it," Luke whimpered.

"If they're dead, it's because of you!"

"No," he pleaded.

"It was months, Luke."

He looked to the sand.

"You lied to me for months!"

"I only meant for it to—"

"You made me think you were sick, Luke."

"I only hoped we—"

"No, Luke. No. I don't want any more of your lies."

"I'm not lyin' now!"

She was about to respond, but cut herself short, and then turned away. She walked off.

"No, sis," Luke cried, running after her. He grabbed at her arm, but she shrugged him off.

"Go away!" she screamed.

"I'm sorry, sis!" he bellowed, the tears flooding his face. "Please don't go." He pawed at her, but she pushed him back. He stumbled after her again, slipping as he went. She shoved him harder, until he was left splayed in the sand. He got up, but Nox held him back.

"Let her go," he said. "Let her cool off."

The boy turned to him. "This is your fault!" he shouted.

Nox sighed.

"You told me to tell her!" Luke came at him, hammering his fists on Nox's chest. "You made me tell her. You made me." He kicked at Nox's shins, but Nox just stood there, taking the beating.

All the while, that seemingly sympathetic sun was growing a little fiercer, smiling a little broader. Sometimes the land didn't have to get you. You got yourself.

Chapter Seventeen

LETTIN' THE MOMENT PASS

L uke sat with his back against the monowheel, cross-armed and scowling. Nox sat farther away. He knew he had to give the boy some space to cool off as much as the boy needed to do the same for his sister. No one was happy. He would've liked to have said that was the product of a lie, but he kind of felt maybe it was from the truth.

"I'm sorry it worked out that way," Nox said.

Luke responded with a glare.

"I'm sure it'll be fine," Nox added. He hoped that wouldn't turn out to be another lie.

Luke's face shifted between anger, sorrow, and guilt.

"She'll be back in—"

"I'm not talkin' to you," Luke said.

"Fair enough."

"You made everything worse."

That was the problem with the truth. It might've been the right thing to do, but sometimes a lie helped more. Some of the best lies were the ones you told yourself. If you spent too much time dwelling on the truth in Altadas, you'd go mad. There were many walking testaments to that.

"I meant to make it better," Nox said.

Luke looked at him. "Yeah, well, there's what you mean and what you do."

If this were a gunfight, that'd be a killing shot. Then again, sometimes the gun backfired, so you had to be careful what you loaded it with. That kid had filled a whole six-shooter full of lies. It was only a matter of time before someone got hurt.

Nox said nothing. He let the kid have that little win. He needed it, though it didn't do much to make up for that big loss. Nox couldn't count the amount of times he had to indulge one of his own kids after they'd fallen out. Siblings had a way of loving and hating each other with equal force. Sometimes it took a few hours to change, or a few days. Then everything'd be back to normal—until the next swing of the pendulum.

But not this.

It took a while for either of them to notice, and it was the boy who spotted it first.

"Her bag," he said.

"Hmm?"

"Her bag!"

Nox looked around. He didn't see it anywhere. That was the problem.

Luke jumped up in a panic. "She took her bag!"

"Relax, boy. She probably just—"

"We have to find her."

By now, Nox was telling little lies of his own, mostly to himself. *She's probably just scouting ahead. She's probably just taking some time away. She's probably just waiting for the anger and hurt to pass.*

But the spectre of truth suggested an alternative: *She's probably just not coming back.*

Chapter Eighteen

THE SEARCH

They wandered out a bit, following the faint trail of Laura's footsteps, but by the time they got a few yards out, the wind was already conspiring against them. It hid her prints and left little decoys in other places, until Nox and Luke were walking in circles.

"We need to find her," Luke said, placing his hand on Nox's forearm. He no longer sounded angry. That pendulum had swung again, and now it was at worry.

"We'll find her," Nox promised, and hated making a promise of it at all. They might find her dead, and it'd still be a promise fulfilled, by letter if not by spirit.

They used the monowheel now, circling the area in ever larger rings. The wind tossed the sand more violently, enough for Nox to don a pair of goggles and give Luke another set. When he heard the boy cough and gag on the desert's debris, he offered him his neckerchief, which the boy tied around his mouth.

Another circle, another empty stretch of land, and another bout of worry. As the sandstorm rose, so too did their concern. Laura was out there, caught in it somewhere, assuming she hadn't already walked off too far. In one way they hoped she hadn't, and in another they hoped she had.

The dunes shifted, and the monowheel plummeted down new drops and climbed up new slopes. The land was playing with them. Nox knew what the tribes would have said about this, that he'd made the land angry, and was paying the price. He needed to make a blood sacrifice. But the land was always angry. And if it needed sacrifices, well, you'd think all those bodies he racked up would count.

The search was fruitless, right up until the point when they came under the shadow of the Rust Valley, where even the sun abandoned its torment. Through the periodic gaps in the shifting walls of sand, they could see the entrance to that horrid place.

Nox parked the monowheel, but kept the engine running. He hoped the hum of it wouldn't lure out more of those metal-hungry clockwork constructs.

"Did she go in?" Luke asked timidly.

Nox scoured the path ahead. It was faint, but he could see footprints. They weren't his, and they weren't Strawman Sanders'. They were a little smaller. Female.

Nox kept his poker face, trying hard not to shake his head or give away any other tell. He'd learned how to do that well when facing down the hunted. He never quite thought he'd be doing this different kind of hunt. The problem was: the prey was likely already dead.

"No," Nox said eventually, hoping he hadn't waited too long. It was a lie, a big, black lie, but the truth had allied with the land. It was an enemy now as well.

"Are you sure?" the boy asked. He lifted his

goggles and stared into the shadows cast by the carcasses of trucks and landships.

"She's not in there," Nox said, telling himself he meant: *She's in Heaven, boy, if there's any space in Heaven for the likes of us.* He always thought he'd go there guns blazing. But now that he was filling his own six-shooter full of lies, he'd probably have to settle for Hell.

Chapter Nineteen

DAMNED IF YOU DO

"I think she might've went this way," Nox suggested, taking them eastward, away from that wretched scrapyard jungle where Laura had disappeared. He knew the boy must've thought he was lying, but maybe he wanted to accept the lie. It was better than the truth.

They passed through the sandstorm again, and out into an open stretch of land. The sun had spent the hours gloating, but now it sank in the west, like a beacon over that silhouette of jagged metal towers.

"It's my fault," Luke said, clinging on behind him.

In a way, it was. In another way, it was Nox's fault. In yet another, it was Laura's. There was no end to the blame. You could deal it out like cards. Everyone came away with a full hand.

Nox couldn't help but feel that the boy clung on a little tighter than before. If Laura was gone, then he had no one left. That was it. The Rust Valley had claimed them all. It'd saved nothing for the maw of the desert.

Nox had no answers for this. He couldn't shoot his way through this problem. He couldn't bash it up like he'd do with some tight-lipped criminal. This was all outside his jurisdiction. He'd left behind the days of being a parent years before, though he hadn't done it willingly. Now the desert gave him another girl and boy, and here it was again, taking them away.

He couldn't let it take both of them.

He drove back to his hideout, his hidden bunker in the plateaus. They travelled through a maze of passages between the granite cliffs, some open, but many barely wide enough for the monowheel to whiz through. When they arrived at the steel door that led into Nox's abode—which was more of a workshop than a home—the boy was asleep in the back.

Good, Nox thought. *Hopefully it's better there, wherever you're dreamin'*. Nox knew it wasn't for him. Even after he'd caught the killers of his family, the nightmares kept on coming. He only got a night of rest when he gunned down the terrors of the day.

Nox tried to open the door quietly, but it clanged and screeched. The boy woke, looking around groggily.

"Where are we?"

"Home," Nox said, though he knew it was not the boy's home. That kid didn't have one.

Luke stretched his arms and jumped out of the back.

Nox turned back to the door, which chugged slowly open.

"We'll rest here tonight," he said. "I'll work up some new trackers and we can search again in the—"

He heard the monowheel engine fire up. He turned, seeing the boy at the wheel. Luke revved, kicking up a plume of dust.

"I have to find her," Luke said, his face full of apologies.

Nox made a dash towards him, but the monowheel sprang away. It rocked uneasily under the boy's control, but the Coilhunter couldn't catch it on foot. He aimed his grappling hook, but knew it wouldn't reach. He tapped at his wristpad, but knew it didn't work if the vehicle was being controlled manually. He watched helplessly as Luke disappeared around a bend, as the desert opened up for a second bite.

Chapter Twenty

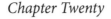

A FAVOUR

Nox raced into his workshop, firing the lights on and shoving open doors. He fumbled through chests of belongings and piles of equipment. The place was a mess, but then he rarely spent time there. That was just where he regrouped, where he took a glance at the toys he once made for his children, and where he made new ones to take down criminals.

He found a makeshift radio. This was one of the few places in Altadas where the Regime wasn't listening in on your calls, but it was also one of the worst places to get a signal. The desert ate that too.

He adjusted the dial, changing one channel of static to another just as bad. You couldn't even pick up the Regime's propaganda broadcasts. You'd have a better chance of getting some of the illegal music stations run by the gangs, though only when close to one of their dens.

Nox tried to amplify the reach, running all manner of wires together, flinching from the shock. The faint electric lights in his bunker flickered momentarily. People'd kill for that kind of technology, and often had. That's why he had to take a leaf out of the criminals' book and hide away.

He forced open several doors, pulling great levers that had almost sealed shut. He raced up steps and slopes, and fired his grappling hook to pull him up a few levels a little quicker. When he came out at the top, he stood on the flat roof of the plateau, where he had a solar-powered generator and a signal dish.

He hooked the radio up to the dish, moving it manually to point in different directions as he tried to find a signal. Then he got it, though it was faint and muddled with static.

"Porridge," he said. He had to say it a few times.

"Oh!" a man replied, his shrill voice cutting through the hiss. "It's you, plum!"

"I need a favour."

"Anything for my little—"

"I need a lift."

"Oh, well! Isn't it a treat that I've got such strong arms, hmm?"

"Your copter," Nox said.

He had no time for pleasantries, and that's almost all Porridge had time for.

"My what?"

"I need you to fly it here."

"Where's *here*?"

"My workshop. Park it on the roof."

"It doesn't really *park*, per se."

"Just be here."

"When do you want me? Oh, when doesn't he!"

"Now, Porridge. I need you now."

"It'll take me an hour, peach. At least that."

"Give it all you've got."

"Oh! You know me!"

Nox turned off the channel and raced back down into his workshop. An hour was plenty of time to do what he needed to do, but it was also plenty of time for Luke to die. He knew where the kid was going, where Laura had already gone. He'd try to catch him before he went inside, but he knew there wasn't much time for that. He'd have to go in after.

He filled a bag with supplies, grabbing some parts from his shelves. There was a lot of unfinished stuff, things he thought he'd have many months to work on, but now couldn't wait. He dragged a heavy chest out from under his barren bed. He took two extra-large revolvers out, which were a little too big for him. He hadn't quite gotten them to work reliably, but when they did, they fired rounds that could pierce metal. He scooped boxes of ammunition into a bag.

He took out his pocket watch. Still half an hour to go. Thirty minutes closer to the boy's death.

He broke into one of the rooms he hadn't touched in a while, a bit of an abandoned project. He thought one day he might need it. He didn't quite expect it'd be so soon. The lights didn't work there, and he had to fight his way through cobwebs.

He lit an oil lantern and opened up a steel cabinet on the far wall. He held the light up. It was very weak, but it was enough to show the huge metal suit of armour inside.

Chapter Twenty-one

COPTER SUPPORT

The Coilhunter was waiting for the copter on the rooftop plateau when Porridge arrived. The rickety flying machine gave the appearance that it flew on belief as much as science. It was orb-shaped, with many glass bubbles across its surface, where the driver could see out into the dusty domain. It had numerous propellers and engines, some of which broke down as it flew, causing the machine to drop, before the next set kicked in, and the entire globe rotated, sending the driver inside towards one of the many other windows. The vehicle kicked up the sand something fierce, and it might've kicked the Coilhunter over the edge of the cliff, were he not like an immovable statue in his new armour.

The copter didn't so much as park as crash. It got as close as it could, then the engines conked out, and it fell like a brick, leaving a little crater in the plateau. One of the many circular doors creaked open, and out stepped Porridge, a tall, thin, somewhat effeminate man with an outrageous style of dress, colourful and gaudy. You rarely caught him in the same clothes or colours, and if you thought you'd seen all the shades of the rainbow, Porridge had a few hundred more just for himself.

On this particular day, he was all silk scarves, wrapped around his abdomen and arms as much as his neck, and in various pastel hues. His playful golden curls slipped through a variety of tied scarves that formed a kind of headdress. Just like you rarely saw Nox without his cowboy hat, you rarely saw Porridge without one of his thousand equivalents.

"Oh!" Porridge cried, frolicking over to Nox, who didn't move an inch. "I'm here! I'm here!"

"Good," Nox said, marching towards the vehicle with a clang in his step. Porridge tried to link his arm, but couldn't quite get his own around the immense plating that now protected the Coilhunter.

"Oh my," Porridge said. "You've grown, pickle."

Nox's boots made an even louder clang when they hit the metal floor of the copter. It was significantly harder to move in his new armour. He was sacrificing mobility for survivability. Sometimes you had to do that, or you'd be sacrificing yourself instead.

Porridge trotted after him, making fainter footsteps with his high heels. Nothing about him was for agility or practicality. He was an odd remnant of the days when people didn't have to think about survival when it came to clothing.

"I'm in a hurry," Nox said.

"I can see that," Porridge replied, trying to squeeze past him. He hurried to the pilot's chair, which was attached to a metal track. It allowed the seat to swing back and forth in multiple directions, from one globular window to another. It had to. That vehicle didn't so much as fly as roll across the sky like a tumbleweed.

The eccentric pilot started the engines up, and the propellers spun like crazy outside. The metal groaned, steam spewed, and one or two rivets pinged out of their holdings. The whole thing looked and felt like it was about to fall apart at any moment. It was as mismatching as its owner's attire.

"Oh, my ripened raspberries!" Porridge exclaimed.

"What's wrong?"

Porridge glanced back at Nox in his colossal armour.

"How much does that weigh?" he shrieked.

"A lot."

"This is going to slow us down."

Nox grumbled. "Can't you adapt?"

Porridge glanced around at his collection of, in his words, doodads and doohickeys. A lot of the stuff had nothing to do with the copter at all. "I can try," he squeaked.

"Try harder."

Anyone else might've been more polite to someone doing them a favour, but Nox knew Porridge owed him big time, and there was no time for pleasantries. He only hoped what little time there was would be enough to save Luke. He'd already given up hope for Laura. That hourglass was well and truly spent.

It took a tremendous effort to get the copter off the ground, and Nox didn't think that it was entirely due to the added weight. It wouldn't be the first time it was overburdened. Porridge had made a living out of scavenging, and there was no greater scavenging ground than the Rust Valley. He was one of the few people brave enough, or mad enough, to hover over that place. You had to be mad to fly one of these things. You had to be even madder to fly it over Clockwork Commune territory.

Nox got to work on some things of his own. His suit wasn't quite finished, but he felt he needed more than just good armour. He never went into a fight without a few extra toys, and he thought he'd need more than a few for this. He took off one of his shoulder pads and screwed a few wooden and metal panels together. He caught the periodic glances of Porridge, and couldn't help but wonder if he was looking at him or salivating over the gadgets in his hands.

"So, plum … what is this all about?"

"It's a rescue mission."

Porridge eyed him up and down, making a variety of expressions—far more than necessary. "Are you sure you're not readying to fight a war, hun?"

"I don't fight wars."

Porridge indulged him with a nod. "You probably should. You're a bit of a one-man army."

Nox shoved the shoulder pad back into place. "Yeah, well now I've got the armour for it."

Chapter Twenty-two

THE ROCKY SKIES

It took longer to get to the Rust Valley by air than Nox had hoped, and he spent much of the time going back and forth between working on his gadgets and gazing out one of the nearby windows. He could feel the grains of sand, like life, slipping away.

And then, just as he was in the middle of some careful mechanics that required him to take off his enormous gloves, the copter shook violently, almost toppling him to the floor.

"What's up?" he asked.

"We're here," Porridge said. "The Rust Valley."

The Coilhunter should've known it by the sudden darkness. Those towers of junk obscured the sun, giving the rust-covered denizens inside an almost perpetual night. The lack of heat was a godsend, especially in Nox's extra protective layers, but the thing about the Rust Valley was: God wouldn't send you in there. But he didn't stop you either. Maybe the Clockwork Commune had shred him too.

"Let me see where we should land," Nox said. He leant against one of the glass bubbles, peering down into the streets of shadows. He heard a sudden crack as a fissure appeared in the glass.

"I wouldn't lean on that, tulip," Porridge warned.

Nox pulled himself up, but heard the rest of the vessel groan. It seemed he couldn't really lean on anything at all.

"It's hard to see," he said.

"Welcome to the Rust Valley. I'd put on the lights, but ... well, you know."

"We might attract company."

"Not that you're not ready for that," Porridge said, biting his lip.

The copter shook even more violently, forcing Nox to grab the netting that held an assortment of scavenged goods to one of the walls.

"Oh!" Porridge cried. "Peach, we have a problem."

The vehicle sank suddenly, tilting as it went, which was enough to cause the pilot seat to swing down upon its track, with Porridge screaming as it went. Nox clung to the net, but the rivets holding it in place started to come away. With each degree the vessel tilted, another rivet popped from the wall, and more of the netting's contents tumbled out. Nox started to slide down the floor towards the cracked window.

The Coilhunter didn't need to ask Porridge what was happening. He could feel it from the vehicle. Something was pulling them in. In the Rust Valley, that could only mean one thing: the Clockwork Commune. There was no doubt the cogs had turned their eyes wide open at the sight of so much metal hovering across the heavens.

Then the netting tore completely, sending Nox down on the glass. He crashed through it, unable to grab a hold of anything, falling down several metres to the cracked ground beneath. In the process of the fall, he saw a series of wires attached to the bottom of the copter, slowly reeling it in.

He turned, spotting the operator of one of those wires. It was a small construct, wheel-shaped, with several large prongs inserted into the ground for stability. It coiled the wire around its entire rust-covered body. It didn't appear to have a face, but it turned slightly towards Nox, as if it noticed him.

The Coilhunter made a dash towards it, thundering across the path. The creature gave a shriek like metal grating against metal. Nox unleashed a dagger from his belt, diving towards the construct. He sliced at the wire, severing it, and knocked the creature on its side from the force of his charge. He came down upon it, just in time to grasp some of the metal prongs that now stabbed wildly at him. Had he been in his normal cloth and leather, they would have impaled him. Now, they just battered off the plating, making a little percussive tune, a little like the ones he sometimes played on his guitar to frighten enemies.

Nox grasped any part of the creature he could get a hold of and yanked it free, tearing it piece by piece. It didn't quite have limbs, so that'd have to do. And it did. The creature slumped to the ground in a pile of springs and cogs, the guts of the living machines.

But this was only one of them. The others continued to haul the copter in, despite Porridge's best efforts to keep it airborne. The propellers on one side severed another wire, but they broke down in the process, forcing the vessel to rotate in the air as the next set took the dominant position. The rotation pulled two of the constructs up from the ground. Nox saw them cast high, then swing like pendulums. Each of them was different, though they all had similar wheel shapes.

Porridge couldn't hold out much longer. The copter struck the top of one of the scrap piles, knocking one of the vehicle remains to the ground. The last of the engines conked out and the vessel careened down, striking the ground and skidding across in a plume of dust, halting just metres away from Nox, who stood unmoving.

One of the hatches swung open, and out stumbled Porridge, his scarves affray. He took a few unsteady steps forward, then turned to look at his vessel. To him, it was more than just a transport. It was home.

"My baby," he said.

"You'll have another one," Nox said.

Then the two constructs that had been pulled up and then down with the copter appeared from either side of the metal orb. Before they could advance, and before Porridge could fully utter his shriek, the Coilhunter grabbed his pistols and gunned them down with his new metal-piercing ammunition.

Porridge hurried up to the Coilhunter, clutching his scarves as he went.

"Wait with the copter," Nox told him. "Get it back up and runnin'."

"But I don't feel safe here."

Nox looked at him. "Good, because you're not."

Chapter Twenty-three

OWL-LIGHT TRACKING

The Coilhunter headed into the maze. The thing about the Rust Valley was that as soon as you entered it, you were already lost. How the Clockwork Commune found their way, no one knew. Anyone who did was quickly added to another scrapyard pile, this time of flesh and bone.

Nox surveyed the area. It wasn't much to look at. There were various winding paths between the high walls of crushed cars. It was hard to see far, as the walls blocked his view, and the shadows they cast made it difficult to see. His own mask, which now extended over all of his face, also added to the obscuration.

He pressed a little latch on his right shoulder pad, which opened the circular hatch made into the armour. Out of it came a tightly-folded, spring-loaded set of wood and steel panels, which opened as they sprang into the air, forming into the shape of an owl. It fluttered there for a moment, before intense headlights shone out from its large, circular eyes. Nox shielded his own.

Nox yanked a panel open on the inside of his left wrist. He'd moved his wristpad to there, thinking it might be safer there, away from the prodding and stabbing of the Clockwork Commune. He entered a few commands. There weren't many he could give this new toy. It wasn't a fighter or a transport, or even a tracker. It was just another set of eyes, up in the sky.

As Nox bashed the controls, he thought about the monowheel the kid took. He could still control it now, and bring it back to him, but he was afraid that he might bring it back alone, and leave the boy stranded wherever he was. Then again, if the kid was stranded in the afterlife, there wasn't much the Coilhunter could do. He hadn't quite made the right toys for that.

The owl ascended up past the pinnacles of the junk barriers, making it look like there were two moons out. Its light grew fainter on the ground the farther it went up, but it was better than nothing—and better than the daylight that never entered that place. The sun was all kinds of cruel, but it was also several shades of wise.

Nox tried to track the monowheel, but its signal was weak. He hadn't quite considered the possibility that the Clockwork Commune might be using signal jammers, or that those jammers might be little walking constructs of their own. He hadn't prepared for that. He didn't have the time to prepare. Even now, he didn't just feel the hourglass emptying—he felt it cracking. You couldn't fill it back up with the sand of the desert. That stuff was only there to kill you, not give you an extra lease of life.

He directed the owl to lead a path for him, well aware that it wasn't just guiding his way. It was acting like a beacon for the denizens of the Rust Valley, telling them where he was. In any other situation, that was madness—and he wasn't altogether sure it wasn't madness now. But if it helped direct their attention away from the boy, and away from the lucrative scrap-ball that Porridge was hiding in, then the Coilhunter could live with that. The question was: for how long?

Chapter Twenty-four

THE CONGREGATION

The Coilhunter turned a corner and found himself in a large clearing, still shrouded in shadow, though now illuminated by the eyes of his own clockwork owl. It showed many things. Some of them were still, the bones of people. And some of them were moving, the limbs of constructs. They reared their ugly heads to stare at this new arrival, so full of gleaming metal. They hadn't found much in the bodies of those unlucky souls that scattered the area, though one or two had made off with a necklace or a pocket watch. The Coilhunter, on the other hand, was a walking prize. They could do a lot with all those metal platings. As for the rest of him, well—at least he'd have company amongst the bones.

He stared them down, not with his uncovered, vulnerable eyes, but through the metal gauze of his helmet. The owl illuminated his glare. Nobody moved. Like the calm before the storm, there was the stillness before the draw. He didn't wonder who would stir first. He knew it'd be him.

He wondered if they knew fear, and thought that maybe if they didn't, he could teach them it, like he'd taught manners to the foul-tongued and the red-handed. These were an uncultured race, a product of the discarded. If the Wild North were a living place, as the local tribes often claimed, then these were the embodiment of its dark subconscious. The spirits of men could haunt you, so why would the spirits of machines be any different?

He could see a few of the constructs shifting slightly, reaching out slowly with their mismatching limbs, hoping he didn't notice. But he saw them. He saw them as clear as he saw the twitch of a finger readying to pull out a gun.

He drew and fired, just as the first of the constructs readied to leap his way. The armour-piercing bullets, a product of the war down south, punctured great big holes in them, tearing through their clockwork innards, sending them down to join the human dead. He fired again, and again, moving his arms in an arc, crossing his arms over each other, before moving them back again. He blew off metal limbs and metal heads, and left that iron congregation with everything to pray for, but no one there to pray.

The people Nox faced gave him names by the dozen, and maybe the constructs would do the same. In the Rust Valley, he wasn't just another victim, another flesh-covered soul in a world of metal. He'd made their most coveted metals his armour, and one by one he'd gunned them down, as if they were flesh and blood. Maybe they'd called him the Rustkiller, and fear him just as much as the other peoples of the Wild North.

This was a test of if it all worked in action. As he surveyed the scattered parts and broken pieces, he felt he'd passed.

Chapter Twenty-five

MORE SCRAP FOR THE HEAP

Luke hadn't found his sister. When he travelled into the Rust Valley on the monowheel, full of drive and passion, a large part of him believed that he'd find Laura. That part of him was growing smaller now.

The monowheel was fast, far faster than he expected, and he had trouble holding on. The engine roared beneath him, as if it knew he was not its master. He felt his bones rattle inside his skin. When the vehicle tilted this way and that, he almost closed his eyes, expecting it to topple over completely. He didn't have the body weight to push it back. It seemed to adjust on its own from some interior balancing mechanism. He knew he was lucky it was the Coilhunter's vehicle. Others weren't made with so much care.

But the thing about luck in the Wild North was that it was usually bad. Like most things there, any sliver of good luck you got ran out quick. Just like the fuel inside the monowheel.

The vehicle stuttered and slowed, before it conked out entirely. Luke banged his fist off the chassis, partly out of frustration, partly out of remembering what he'd seen most men do in similar situations. Just like those times, it didn't do much good.

And then it got worse. Without the movement of the wheel, which was linked to the balancing mechanism inside, gravity got a hold of it and began to pull it down. Luke tried to kick the stand out, but it wouldn't budge. He hopped off and tried to prop the monowheel up with his body, but the weight of it was immense, and it just made his feet skid across the sand. He yelped as he threw himself out of the way as the whole thing came crashing down on its side.

He sat where he landed for a moment, wondering what he was doing here. This was precisely the place he didn't want to be, and instead of being here with his sister, or with the Coilhunter, he was alone. He thought maybe he deserved it. He was a fraud. Maybe Nox should have had a poster with his face on it too.

But there was no time for self-pity. He knew his sister was still out there, somewhere in this maze. He blocked out logic, which said there were too many paths she could have taken. He only let hope and perseverance through.

He got up and grabbed a hold of the wheel. He leant back, trying to let his body weight haul the vehicle upright. It was hopeless. It barely moved an inch. He circled around it, scratching his head. He didn't like the idea that he'd have to walk the rest of the way. He hadn't even considered what the Coilhunter might do to him if he didn't get his monowheel back.

He wondered if the vehicle might be able to right itself if it had more fuel. He saw the diesel canisters on either side of the box at the back. One of them was pinned between the monowheel and the ground, but the other was free. Luke grabbed a hold of its handle and tried to yank it free, but just like everything else with that vehicle, it weighed a ton. It took everything he had, with both hands on the canister and both feet pressed against the hull of the vehicle, to dislodge it. When he did, he fell backwards with it, and the canister leapt from his hands, crashing on the ground. The lid burst and the oil spilled out.

"No!" the boy cried, racing over to it and pulling up the almost empty canister. He shook it, hearing the barely audible slosh of a dribble of liquid inside. It wasn't enough. If you had a water canister like that, those last few drops wouldn't do much to stave off death. These last few drops of diesel wouldn't do much either.

He looked at the pool of oil in front of him, winding its way between the cracks, running away from him. He felt a different fuel well inside him, and he swung the canister away with a shout. It bounced, casting away its final droplets. He clenched his fists and stomped the ground. Then he grabbed a metal bar that stuck out from one of the nearby piles of debris and tossed it across the way, where it clanged off one of the scrapyard walls.

He sat back down, panting. He wanted to scream at the top of his voice, but he knew it'd do no good. Nothing he'd done so far had done any good. His mother used to tell him he had to find a way to channel his anger. He thought of Nox and how he'd channelled his. He wondered why he couldn't do it, why he kept choosing the wrong path, doing the wrong things. It just made him angrier. He tried to hide it, tried to bury it, but it just came out worse than ever.

Then he heard a sudden ping of metal, and he started. He glanced around rapidly, expecting to see one of the Clockwork Commune. Instead, he saw the little hatch open at the back of the monowheel. The small ramp extended and the wind-up duck waddled down, halting at the end.

"No. Go back inside!" He shooed it with his hands, but the little duck just looked at him blankly. Luke paused and bit his lip. "You're gonna blind me, aren't you?"

The duck didn't move. Its beady eyes didn't blink, and yet they almost seemed like they could see. He didn't know how the Coilhunter did it. Maybe it came to him like the drawings did to Luke, through some higher inspiration. Maybe if there was some divine power, that was how it spoke to the world. Or maybe they were both just crazy.

Luke didn't try to run. He was tired of running. If the duck killed him, then that would be the end of it. He didn't want to die, but at least it would kill the anger too.

The duck tilted its head away. It seemed to be staring off in the direction where he'd thrown the iron bar.

"What?" Luke asked. "Do you see somethin'?"

The duck kept staring.

Luke felt suddenly on edge.

He got to his feet slowly.

"What is it?" he whispered, unsure why he even

asked. Could the duck even speak?

Luke looked where the duck was staring. He couldn't see anything but the usual metal junk. The entire place was an iron graveyard. You could barely take a step without hitting a grave. He didn't like that thought right now, because now he wondered if he might find his own.

He felt suddenly defenceless. He glanced around, spotting another iron bar sticking out from one of the walls. He yanked it free, though in the process it loosened many other random metal bits, which toppled to the ground with a clash and clang.

He cringed at the sound, backing away slowly.

Then he thought he heard something else.

His eyes darted in the direction the duck looked. He gulped. Then, as he watched, he thought he saw part of the wall move. He clenched his mouth to stop his gasp. What at first looked like just another part of the wall far ahead now turned to him. It was tall and black, and hunched over. It seemed to have half a head, with just one eye, which glared at him with a kind of intensity he had never seen. He thought he knew anger, but this thing knew hate.

Chapter Twenty-six

BOYS DON'T DIE

L uke stood motionless, until the construct shifted. The boy flinched, dropping the iron bar on the ground. In his head, he'd envisioned bashing the creature, but now that it came to it, he knew he couldn't really fight it. He had to run.

The creature bounded forward, half-limping, half-leaping. It seemed that one of its legs didn't work properly, so it had to drag it along behind it. Yet even then it moved at a tremendous speed.

Luke raced in the other direction, panting, and trying hard to contain his scream. He jumped over piles of rubble, tripping and tumbling, before dashing off again. He skidded around a corner, barely able to stop himself, and then halted suddenly in front of a wall of metal.

It was a dead end.

He looked around frantically, trying to spot some little crevice to squeeze through, but the walls were packed tight. He couldn't even wiggle through the door of a vehicle, because they were all crushed together under the tremendous weight.

He heard the creature rattle behind him, and then it gave a terrible wail that sounded like nothing Luke had ever heard in his life. He'd heard the other kids tell tales of these creatures, of how you heard their howls at night before they took you away. It brought back his childhood terrors and mixed them with the horrors of the moment.

He tried to climb the wall of junk. There were lots of jutting bits to grab and stand on, but many were sharp, and others shifted under his weight. As he clambered up, breathing frantically, he heard the whole wall groan, like a wail of its own.

Then he heard the little duck's quack, and he barely had time to brace himself against the wall when everything exploded into blinding white. His eyes burned, even more than the last time, because now they went from the dark of the Rust Valley to the light of the Coilhunter's weapon. He clenched his teeth and held on tight. He couldn't see anything, not the jutting iron bars and steel beams, not the crumpled hulls of vehicles, not even his hands. He could feel it, the coarse, sharp edges, the rusty patches, the rivets and screws.

He wasn't sure what to do, to drop back down or continue his climb, or to just stay there, clinging onto the metal as if it were life. He hoped the construct was also blind, but he knew what his mother had said about how differently they saw. The duck couldn't distinguish between man and machine, so it tried to blind them equally.

But it was not equal.

He heard something dragging across the ground beneath him. He tried to hold his breath, to silence those loud pants and heaves. He felt his hand almost slipping and had to adjust. The wall groaned, as if to give him away.

Don't notice me, he prayed. *Don't see me. I'm not here, I'm not here, I'm not here.*

Then the construct wailed.

It saw him just fine.

Luke reached up, feeling his way for the next thing to hold. He grabbed at something, like the edge of a door. He hauled himself up, then felt his foot slip as something gave way beneath him. He cried out, dangling for a moment before he managed to get a foothold on something else. He reached up again, but felt nothing but air, and then the sheer, slippery side of a chassis. There was nothing to grab onto.

Yet for the construct below, there was plenty. It reached up with its three-fingered hand and seized the boy by the ankle.

Luke shrieked. He tried to kick it off, but the grip was firm.

Then it pulled.

Luke felt his own fingers strain and buckle. He screamed at the top of his lungs. He let go, but caught something else, and kept flailing his legs below him, trying to shake that iron grip.

Then it pulled harder, and he came tumbling down to the ground. He clattered off the side of the creature's torso and rolled to the ground with a thud, landing on his back. He groaned as he lay there, battered and bruised, and still very blind.

He heard something stab the ground beside his head, tearing a little whimper from him. Then something leant close to him, close enough that he could hear the ticking inside its shell. He knew this was it. This was the end. This was why he didn't want to come here.

Then his vision started to return. He blinked rapidly as the white became less blinding. He saw the silhouette hovering over him. There was no doubt what it was. It was the lumbering construct, there to add another set of bones to its belt of trophies.

The creature raised its barbed arm to strike, and Luke raised his own to shield his face.

Chapter Twenty-seven

THUNDER

The gunshot was like thunder. The construct never even wailed. It never had a chance to. Even though Luke could still only see in silhouettes, he could see through the gigantic hole in the creature's head. It slumped down on top of him, halting mere inches from his face. He climbed out from under it and got to his feet.

Even in silhouette, you could recognise him. Even though now he seemed bulkier than before, Luke could spot the Coilhunter. It was as if he had already drawn an outline in the journal of his mind. It was a reassuring shape in a world of shadows and jagged edges.

"So, *here* you are," Nox said, his voice as full of grit as ever, though now it seemed even more muffled than before. Luke tried not to think of how that must've sounded to the bad guys, and tried even harder not to think that maybe now, in the eyes of the Coilhunter, he might be one of them.

The boy looked to the ground, ashamed. When the image of the Coilhunter grew clearer, he saw that awful visage, now encased in its own iron shell, as if he'd joined the Clockwork Commune. It stopped the boy's breath and locked away the words fighting at the back of his throat.

The duck waddled up to the Coilhunter's foot and looked up at him, and then back to the boy. Nox looked down at it.

"And here *you* are," he added. He flicked open a panel on the inside of his wrist and pressed a button. The duck waddled back to the fallen monowheel and climbed inside.

"I hope you're not mad," Luke said.

"I thought you were the one who was mad."

"I was, but—"

"But now you're not?"

"I don't know what I am." Luke could feel his eyes welling up. "I just want to find my sister."

The Coilhunter's shoulders rose and fell noticeably, and a puff of black smoke came out from his mask.

"This'll get ya killed, boy."

Luke nodded slightly.

"This'll get *me* killed."

Luke thought it better not to nod to that.

"I'm not leavin'," Luke said. He thought maybe that was a stupid thing to say. Most people wouldn't care if he left or not—and yet here was the Coilhunter. He wasn't like most people at all. "I'm not leavin' without her."

The Coilhunter stared at him for a moment, and Luke stared back, defiant. He quickly rubbed a stray tear away, a little betrayal in this war of wills. Most people never got to fight a war with the Coilhunter and win. But then most people never walked the Rust

Valley.

Nox spun his revolver, and Luke flinched. Then he holstered it and turned to the monowheel.

"You made a right mess outta that."

"Sorry."

"Let's hope you're as good at destroying the Clockwork Commune."

Luke perked up. "So, you mean you'll help me find her?"

"Come on, boy," Nox said, starting off. "Before I change my mind."

Chapter Twenty-eight

THE CULTURE CACHE

They wandered for what felt like hours, meeting no more metal monsters, contenting themselves with the monsters in their imagination. It was hard not to look at the scrapyard walls and see faces in the shapes, and then glance again and find it was just some junk.

The owl scouted the way for them, shining its twin spotlights on the refuse of the war that waged across Altadas. Those burnt-out vehicles, those trampled trucks, those blasted landships. They all ended up here. Some said the Regime sent them. Others said it was the Resistance. Others yet said they both conspired together, making this little offering to the Clockwork Commune, keeping them at bay.

"Nox." Luke tapped a bar in his hand as he went. Every few yards, he threw it away and picked up a new one.

"Yeah?"

"Are we gonna die out here?"

"If you mean the Wild North … then … some day."

"Today?"

"No."

"How're you so sure?"

"You're with me, boy. How're you not?"

Luke dropped the iron bar and found yet another one. There was no shortage of them here. They were like guns were to the other parts of the Wild North. There were more of them than hands to hold them. The boy cringed at the sound of the metal hitting the debris below. It seemed he never quite thought that through. But it seemed he hadn't quite thought through coming here either. That was the problem with many. Hell, the problem with most. Everyone was caged by the here and now. Well, here and now was enough to think about.

They continued through the winding passages, stumbling into dead ends, trotting after the owl when it seemed to fly off more suddenly, or braving the dark when it slowed down too much. Nox gave the boy one of his metal gauntlets to replace the next iron bar, which let the Coilhunter make some small adjustments to his wristpad with one of his tools. He couldn't be all things to all people. Right now he needed to be a mechanic. But when he faced those constructs again, he needed to be a killer. An armoured one.

"Look at this!" Luke cried, casting aside the glove and racing over to a fallen hot air balloon. It draped over one of the smaller piles of junk, with its basket on its side. The contents were sprawled across the ground.

Luke picked up a painting that was almost as big as him. There was a tear in the canvas, but you could still see the picture well. It looked like an old noble, staring off to the side. You couldn't see where he was staring, because it no longer existed. Those days were gone. Likely, that man was gone too.

"Isn't it pretty?" Luke asked.

Nox strolled over to his discarded glove and scooped it up. "Yeah, I guess."

"Why's it in here? Surely they wouldn't throw it out."

"It's supposed to be in the sky, boy. A culture cache, a saving for a rainy day." Nox smirked at the notion. There weren't many rainy days in the desert. "The Clockwork Commune must've pulled it down, searchin' for metal."

Luke looked around at the discarded artworks. "I guess they didn't find any."

"No."

Luke dusted off the bottom right-hand corner. The painting had a signature, but it was badly faded. That was probably a good thing. Signatures on art were like signing your own death warrant, at least when it came to the Iron Empire, or, as the Resistance called them, the Regime. That was why people came up north. You could do the things here that you just couldn't do elsewhere, and get away with it. That meant the good, and the very bad. All of it was bad in the eyes of some, and good in the eyes of others. People left their morals on the borders of the Wild North. The Coilhunter taught them new ones.

"Who do you think he is?" Luke asked, propping the painting up against a junk heap. He stood back and rubbed his chin philosophically.

Nox glanced at the lush red silk the figure in the

painting wore, with its fine gold trim. "Treasury, no doubt."

"You think?"

"Well," Nox said, "what the Treasury was before."

"What were they before?"

"The old royalty. Old nobility."

"That must've been nice."

"Yeah. For them."

Luke sighed. "This shouldn't be here. It's not junk."

"Neither should we, boy. We ain't junk either."

"Maybe we could—"

"No. We're gonna look for your sister. One last loop. One last look."

Luke hung his head.

It dawned on Nox that the boy might've been looking for a small distraction, a little bit of light in the darkness. He likely knew just as well as Nox did that his sister was probably dead. Looking for hope was like looking for a needle in all those grains of sand. But despair? Well, that was the sand itself.

Luke placed the painting delicately into the basket, then quickly scooped up the other items to add in too. Nox caught him slipping what looked like an ornate pen into his satchel, but he said nothing. In a land of crime, those little crimes didn't matter. Hell, the boy was right. It was a crime that culture was consigned to the scrap heap, and an even bigger one that it was safer there. Luke dragged the balloon fabric over the basket, protecting it from the weather.

"Do you think it'll be all right?" he asked Nox as he trotted up beside him.

"It ain't iron," Nox said.

"That's good, right?"

"Here, yes."

"But it'll be all right?"

Nox stopped suddenly.

"Nox?"

The owl's lights went dark.

The Coilhunter didn't need to say anything. They both thought it. The art would be all right.

But we won't.

Chapter Twenty-nine

THE IRON GUNSLINGER

The Coilhunter felt it in his gut more than he saw it with his eyes. Something was hunting them. Something was on the prowl. He didn't know what it was, only that it might as well have posters with their faces on them, with that sweet seal of death: the word Reward.

"Back away slowly, boy."

Luke looked up at him, but said nothing.

"Slowly," Nox repeated. "Make it damn slow."

Nox didn't move at all. He didn't reach for his guns. He didn't dive or dodge, didn't cast orbs from his belt, or command a duck to quack. He stood like a statue, like just another piece of scrap in the Rust Valley.

Luke did as he was told, for once. He backed away, real slow—though Nox knew he was itching to make it quick. If he did, that'd be the death of him. Hunters liked their prey to run. Nox knew that all too well.

Nox kept his hands hovering at his sides, ready to draw, yet knowing well that his new suit of armour made him slow. You couldn't afford to be slow in a gunfight. There was the guy who drew fast, and then there was the dead. The dead didn't draw at all.

Then it appeared.

The Coilhunter was taken aback, though he tried not to show it. He'd seen a lot of things in the Wild North, but he hadn't quite seen this. It was almost the mirror image of him, a gunslinger made out of scrap, with a sheet of metal forming the rim of his cowboy hat. Nox had met Iron Ike of the Deadmakers, a construct bounty hunter, dry as the desert, but damn good with a shotgun. But this was something different. This wasn't made for hunting criminals. This was made for him.

Nox waited, studying his opponent. It was bulky, just like him, though its bulk was not just a shell. It was as mismatching as the rest of the Clockwork Commune, a product of whatever was around. From the many staring eyes across the construct's body, it was clear that several other constructs had given themselves up—or been forced to—in order to create this beast.

He heard Luke's faint patters as he retreated, so Nox took a few slight steps of his own to mask the sounds. The clang of his boots reverberated through the scrapyard canyon. The Iron Gunslinger made a few answering movements of its own.

"Stand down," Nox said, "or I'll make ya sit."

He had no idea if his normal intimidation would work on this. It had a body of sorts, even if it was mangled, and appeared to have a mind, even if it seemed to be focused on only one thing. It wasn't clear if it had a soul, or a conscience. Then again, it wasn't clear if most men had those either.

The Iron Gunslinger said nothing. There was a form of intimidation in its silence, in its unmoving form, in its unending glare.

Nox paid special attention to the construct's guns. By the looks of them, they were real. They had little stamps on the handles, suggesting they were made by human hands. No doubt the Clockwork Commune had pried them from those hands, and maybe used them as trophies. They were smaller guns than Nox's, and by the make of them, he could guess that they only carried normal flesh-piercing rounds. You didn't want to get that guess wrong.

Nox waited until he couldn't hear the boy's footsteps any longer. Then he struck. He drew his right pistol and fired, but, like a mirror, the Iron Gunslinger did the same. The bullets crossed over each other, and knocked away the pistols from each other's hands. Nox's spun off into the air and landed by one of the scrapyard walls. No bother. He had another.

He wondered if it was copying him, and yet it matched his movements almost at the same time. He was studying it, but he knew it was studying him. He could see the two glaring eyes under the brim of its hat, but he hadn't considered the many other eyes across the construct's body, watching for all those other little movements. The Clockwork Commune hadn't just made a version of him—it'd made a better one.

"I ain't here for war," the Coilhunter croaked. "I'm just here for my kind."

He wondered if the construct questioned just

what kind that was. He was human hiding beneath a shell of metal. Or maybe it wasn't thinking that at all. Maybe it was just wondering how to flay the iron skin so it could wear it for its own.

Nox hadn't paid much heed to the stories of the Clockwork Commune. He'd heard all sorts of ghost stories from the barflies, and overheard others from the dirt-alley kids of the Burg. How the constructs had no faces, so they took the ones from people. How they stole away naughty children and made them part of the scrapyard walls. He even saw a kid once stick out his tongue as proof that he wasn't a construct, because constructs apparently didn't have any tongues. Somewhere among all the stories, there was probably a hint of truth, and maybe even something helpful in defeating them. But, just like him and Luke, it was lost among the junk.

Then the Iron Gunslinger drew on him. It caught him off guard, and if he wasn't wearing armour, that would've been the end of him. Two bullets pinged off the plating. The construct watched this with great interest. Then Nox fired a single round at the creature's head. It left a hole there, right in one eye, but the creature kept on standing, and kept on staring with the others.

It's learnin', Nox thought. That wasn't good. It seemed to know too much already.

The Iron Gunslinger dropped its second gun. It knew that was where Nox shined. Then it ran, straight towards him. Nox fired again, blowing a hole in its chest. Then again, clipping its side. Then again, piercing its leg. Then the construct crashed into him and bowled him over. They fell to the ground and rolled about, grabbing and shoving and thrashing.

It was stronger than him. He had a metal shell, but that was all it was. It didn't give him more strength. He didn't have the added power of pistons or the added pressure of tightly-wound springs. He was going on muscle and sinew, and sheer determination. And it wasn't enough.

The construct hauled him up and tossed him away. He crashed into one of the scrapyard walls, which sent a pile of iron rubble down on top of him, as if it was aiding its kin. Nox slumped to the ground, feeling defeated.

Then he saw Luke standing across the way, out in the open, under the glare of the Iron Gunslinger's many eyes.

"Run!" Nox cried. Not slow, not careful. "Run!"

Luke ran, then ducked inside a gap in one of the walls. Nox didn't mean hide, but it'd do. Maybe there wasn't really anywhere to run.

So Nox got back to his feet. If this was a walled-off arena, then he would fight. He couldn't let himself be defeated. He couldn't let another child die under his watch. Not again.

Chapter Thirty

INSIDE THE IRON WALLS

L uke scrambled through the passage inside the scrapyard wall, trying not to make too much noise, and cringing at the thought of all that weight above him, supported by a beam here or a bar there. If he tipped off something, it could all come tumbling down on top of him.

He heard the clatter of steel outside as the Coilhunter struggled with the Iron Gunslinger. He didn't have to see the fight to know how it was going. Nox was losing. He could hear it in the grunts and cries, in the scrape of metal, in the crash of his suit against the ground. It made Luke wonder if he should go back out there, try and find a way to help.

But Nox had told him to run.

Luke continued to crawl through the passage, thankful for this little hideaway from the prying eyes of the Clockwork Commune. The walls had already been stripped of the most useful metals, so perhaps the constructs never thought to look there again, to cast their iron eyes inside the walls. Luke was counting on it. His life depended on it.

He halted for a moment and sat cross-legged in his fortress. He peeped out of a gap in the wall at the fight outside. The Coilhunter had lost part of his left shoulder pad, but now he had the Iron Gunslinger by the throat. He pushed the construct back, until it kicked him in the chest, sending him sprawling. They were both made for guns, but both of them were disarmed.

Luke's eye caught the glimmer of one of Nox's pistols just feet away from his position, almost within reach. The boy was safe, for now, but he knew he had to help the Coilhunter or that wouldn't last. Nox didn't look like he could last much longer either.

The gap was barely big enough to see, let alone reach through. He tried to remember if there were any bigger gaps in the passage he came through, and looked to the passage ahead, where the wall was more tightly packed. There might have been larger holes farther on, but that meant climbing out into the open.

Luke studied the packed junk around the opening. He fiddled with an old copper pipe, dislodging it. The faint light came in a little stronger. He tried to remove a small girder, but it was stuck. He plucked a few small springs out of the way, and then a piece of an engine. The wall shook slightly. He gulped, pausing for a moment until the shudder passed.

Please hold, he prayed. He'd heard about the machine spirits. One kid he knew said they only answered to the tribes, but his friend Max said everyone was their own kind of tribe. Max was gone now. He'd joined his tribe in heaven.

The metal didn't answer. That was good. So long as it was silent, it was stable. It was like what the tribes said about thunder. If the sky was quiet, the spirits there were content. Luke wished he knew more about them, how to appease them.

He tried to reach through the opening now, but it was still too small. If he could've got the girder free, that would give him the space he needed, but it looked like it was holding up too much. There was a badly rusted grille propping up some of the other pieces below, but it seemed to be holding less. It could still unsettle everything, but he thought maybe he could bend it, or just move it slightly.

He tried.

The whole wall creaked in answer.

Please hold, he begged.

He yanked one side of it free.

The wall wailed.

He heard pieces shifting, and then the clatter of some parts falling.

Oh, please hold.

He stopped and closed his eyes tightly. He could still hear the struggle outside, but eventually the closer noises ceased. The wall held.

He didn't realise he was also holding his breath until he was forced to let it out with an all too audible sigh. He covered his mouth with his hand, then peered outside. No one had noticed him. He saw the gun still there, so close.

He pulled the grille back gently and squeezed his arm through. It was a tight fit. He pushed through as far as he could go, right up to his shoulder. The grille pinned him in place, taunting him to pull it free, to topple the mountain. He blocked up the gap now with his body, so he couldn't see anything. He felt around outside for the gun, tapping against bits of metal, grasping at piles of sand.

Then he thought he felt the handle of the gun.

Then something grabbed him by his other shoulder.

He yelled and turned to it.

It was his sister.

Chapter Thirty-one

WITHIN REACH

If Luke's arm wasn't still stuck in the hole, he would've hugged his sister. He didn't have to. She hugged him.

"I'm sorry," he whispered. "I'm so sorry. I didn't mean—"

"I'm sorry too," she replied. "I didn't mean it either. I just got … carried away."

"I know. I do too."

She smiled. It was good to see her smile again, and even better for her to smile at him.

Then the clash of the fight outside brought them back to the moment, and her smile faded.

"He's out there, huh?" Laura asked.

"Yeah."

They looked at each other for a moment.

"He's losin'," Luke said. "We need to help 'im."

"Why's your arm stuck?"

"I, uh, was tryin' to get his gun."

He felt around again, but it was hopeless. In the fright, he thought he might have flicked it away. All he felt now was scrap and sand. He pulled his arm back in, and both of them peered out.

"I don't think we can reach that," Laura said.

Luke hung his head.

"Unless maybe we try to use a stick."

"Or this!" Luke said, holding up the copper pipe he'd taken away earlier. Then he grabbed another long metal object with various prongs on it, which seemed like it might be better for hooking far-away objects. "Or this. Whatever it is."

"Let me try," Laura said. She took the pole and fed it through the opening.

"Careful."

"I am."

She fished around for the gun, tapping off the casing.

"Almost!" Luke exclaimed, covering his mouth as he realised he was being too loud.

Laura fished again. "Just … one … more ..."

Then something rolled in front of the hole and banged into the rod. Laura and Luke gasped and put their backs to the wall. An eye pressed up against the opening and stared inside. The kids tried not to make a stir.

Then the eye disappeared, and they heard the crank of old landship treads as the construct rolled off. They cautiously looked outside, spotting the small creature with its triangular hull, over which old, battered treads were attached. It had a flattened, box-shaped body, a small, square-shaped head, and short arms that ended in pincers. It also had the Coilhunter's gun.

Chapter Thirty-two

FOLLOWIN' THE GUN

When Luke saw that little construct race away with the Coilhunter's gun, he didn't think twice. He scrambled after it, crawling through the passage in the same direction it went.

"Wait!" Laura cried. "Luke!"

She hurried after her brother, and the two of them came out of an opening farther on, where they could witness in full the desperate fight between the Coilhunter and the Iron Gunslinger. Luke froze as he saw Nox pinned to the ground, but Laura grabbed him and pulled him down behind some rubble.

"You'll get us killed," she whispered.

"We have to help him."

"I don't think we—"

"The gun," Luke said. He looked around, spotted the little rolling construct dragging the gun away, then leapt out to chase it.

"Luke!" Laura shouted, charging out after them.

The two ran across an open stretch, and then Nox was thrown in their paths. They halted.

"Get outta here!" he yelled, barely able to roll onto his side. His helmet was badly dinted, so much so that the wire mesh in front of his eyes was starting to come away. His dark eyes were more visible than ever.

Laura grabbed Luke's hand and led him around the edge, close to the wall. The Iron Gunslinger spotted them and started to move towards them, but the Coilhunter forced himself up and grabbed the construct's leg, pulling it to the ground.

The kids continued on, faster than ever, round one corner and then another, following the fleeting glimpses of the gun thief. It hadn't dawned on them that it might be leading them into a trap, or that it might turn the weapon on them. They both knew well that if the Coilhunter died, their chances of survival there died with him.

Then they skidded to a halt as they found themselves in another dead end, this time leading into a small chamber inside one of the scrapyard walls, where the construct had assembled a variety of objects into a ring, like a kind of nest. Among them was the Coilhunter's guide owl.

The construct saw them, its wide eyes seeming wider than ever. It drove towards them, bumping into Luke. It only reached up to about Luke's shoulder.

"Ow!" the boy cried. He kicked at it in return.

Then Laura darted into the nest and grabbed the gun.

The construct saw her, raised both its stumpy arms, then spun around on the spot. It never made any noise, no howl or wail, but it was clearly agitated. It charged at her, but Luke grabbed some scrap and fired it at the creature. It raised its arms again, then sped off, but halted a few yards away.

"We've got it," Laura said. "Let's get outta here."

They were about to run, but Luke looked back. He saw the broken owl, and wondered if they might need that too. He also just didn't like the idea of leaving it there. He ran into the nest and grabbed one wing, just as the rolling construct charged back. It tried to stop him, tried to grab the other tattered wing, but Luke scarpered off, letting the owl drag along behind him.

When they reached the corner, Luke looked back again. His father always told him not to do that, but his mother said looking back was how you stopped making the same mistakes. It was how you learned from history. He saw the construct staring at its half-emptied nest. Then it opened a little door on the front of its torso and pulled out a little bucket of green paint and a small brush. It didn't have a mouth, so it painted a frown on its box-shaped head. It turned to look at them, and it no longer seemed threatening. It just looked sad.

"Wait," Luke said. He wondered if the creature thought of those bits of metal as its children. It made Luke feel really bad.

"Come on, Luke!" Laura called. "We don't have time for this."

If the Coilhunter wasn't in danger, Luke might've stayed, and might've tried to understand this strange creature. His mother said they could be understood. But where was she? Was she just another bit of scrap in one of their nests?

Laura grabbed him by the arm and led him off. They headed back to the arena, where the Iron Gunslinger was again on top of the Coilhunter, now trying to rip off his helmet—or perhaps his head.

The kids ducked behind another pile of rubble. Laura flicked open the barrel.

"Two bullets," she whispered. She knew guns as well as Luke knew pencils. He was glad she was the one making the shot. He knew he'd probably miss.

"Well, what are ya waitin' for?" Luke asked. "Shoot!"

"I can't waste them," Laura said. She peeked out over the debris. Luke joined her, clutching the battered owl in his arms.

"It's there," Luke said. "Shoot it."

But Laura wasn't looking for the Iron Gunslinger. She was looking for the holes inside its frame, where the Coilhunter's previous bullets hadn't seemed to have had an effect. Two more random holes wouldn't stop it.

"It's killin' him!" Luke cried. "Shoot!"

So Laura aimed the gun, propping it up against the rubble. It was big, far bigger than she'd held before, and way too big for her frame. She knew the recoil would be bad. She only hoped the wound would be worse.

She fired.

The bullet whizzed straight towards the construct's neck, tearing through some of the wires. If that were a human, its head would've been hanging off—and it'd be dead. But it wasn't. It looked up at her, and so did Nox.

"The heart!" he shouted.

The Iron Gunslinger tried to charge at Laura, but Nox pulled it back, then pulled at the plating around its chest. If she fired then, it might've got his hand. That didn't matter, so long as it got the creature's heart.

She aimed again.

"This is it," she whispered.

Luke held his breath and prayed.

Then, just as Laura clicked the trigger, something knocked into the back of her. She slipped, and the bullet shot into the sky. She grunted and turned to see the little frowning construct parked behind them, its frown even bigger than before.

Chapter Thirty-three

NO LEAD IN THE BARREL

"You little sandsucker!" Laura roared, striking the construct with the butt of the gun. "You ruined it! You ruined it!" If she had another bullet, she might've fired at it instead.

But she didn't.

She was out.

And the Coilhunter's time was following quick.

Luke peeked out at the battle, where it seemed that Nox knew it was all falling apart. He couldn't even get the words out he wanted to speak. The Iron Gunslinger had him firmly by the throat. His eyes said enough though: *Get outta here! Run! Don't look back.*

"Come on," Laura said, grabbing Luke by the arm. "We have to go."

"We're not leavin' him here."

"We have to."

"We don't. We can … do somethin'. Please."

They argued and tugged at each other, until Luke dropped the battered owl. The little rolling construct looked at them and rubbed off its smile with a paint-stained cloth, before splashing on another frown. They barely noticed it in the heat of the moment. They barely even saw it roll away. They paid no attention to where it went.

The little construct skirted around the edge of the battle, hugging the walls. At times, when the Coilhunter and Iron Gunslinger rolled close, it froze, and tried to appear like part of its surroundings. Other times its head ducked inside its torso, and it shuddered.

It continued on, through the passages the others had came from, back to where the river of oil led like breadcrumbs up to the monowheel laying on its side. The construct rolled up to it, then circled it, then tapped it gently with its clamp-like claw. It often did this, because even it was unsure what was just junk or another sleeping construct.

The monowheel didn't budge. The shape of it reminded the construct of another clockwork being it knew, and it cocked its head to see if maybe it was a relative. It was hard to tell.

It paused, hearing the ticking of its own brain and heart. Those ticks were slowing down. It didn't know how the constructs of flesh felt, but it seemed like they knew fear. It seemed like they knew it better when they were dying.

The construct wiped the paint off its face and left it blank. The little tub of paint inside its torso was running out too. It was a guessing game which would go first. It didn't like to guess.

It darted around the area, collecting bits of useful scrap. Another day, it would have added some of these to its nest. That empty nest. If it could sigh, it would've sighed. It saw the constructs of flesh do it often.

The most useful find was a coil of wire, which it clipped into several lengths. It tied several of these around pipes and hooks on the side of the monowheel, and fixed the other ends to the battered hull of a landship that was half submerged in the sand. It attached some cogs, a crank, and a lever, wrapping some of the wire around, until finally it could get to work.

It pulled the lever, and the cogs rotated one place. All the wires went taut, and the monowheel creaked as it raised a little. It tried again, and it came up more. And again, until the vehicle was upright, resting upon its wide landship treads.

That was part one done, and it was the easy part. The harder part would be getting the two gunslingers to bring their battle here.

Chapter Thirty-four

FISTS AND EYES

Nox continued his struggle, but it shouldn't have been a struggle. He had prepared for this, even if he hadn't had the time he really needed. But it didn't matter. The Clockwork Commune was designed to adapt, and they were adapting fast. He'd barely come up with a plan before their emissary, the Iron Gunslinger, already had a counter for it. That meant Nox needed to adapt as well.

He saw the kids return, hiding behind a barrier. The girl fired, but the shot missed. Something else was happening back there, but he couldn't see it. His eyes were fixed on the red glare of the Iron Gunslinger's.

So he ripped some of them out. While it was strangling him, slowly crushing the reinforced armour around his neck, Nox decided not to try to pull the claws away. He didn't have the strength to match the construct. He had to use guile instead.

That glare gave him an idea.

So he reached up to the creature's face, where he'd already left some bullet holes, and yanked the one remaining eye free, exposing the wires beneath. The construct tried to shake off his hands, then took one of its own away from Nox's throat to swat at the

Coilhunter's gloves.

It missed.

Without those eyes on its head, it was harder to see. It should've been impossible, but it still had more eyes dotted throughout its body. Some of them opened now for the first time. Maybe they were backups. Nox would blot them out just the same.

He reached for one, then quickly switched and grabbed another. Feints weren't just for gunfights. You could use them in a fistfight with a construct as well. He plucked the eye out, then went for the first one again, then pretended to go for another, before returning to yank that first one out as well. The Iron Gunslinger scrambled to grab Nox's arm, but he flitted away like a butterfly.

So it realised that approach was fruitless, and it adapted.

It returned both hands to Nox's throat, squeezing with greater ferocity. Nox could already feel the steel rubbing against his skin. It was only a matter of time before he felt it against the bone as well.

Nox kept tearing out those eyes, one by one, but the creature no longer needed to see. It only needed to keep its hands pressed against his neck, and keep on pressing. But what it didn't know was that the Coilhunter had already resigned himself to his fate. He wasn't plucking out those eyes for his sake. He was doing it so the construct couldn't see Luke and Laura, so it couldn't get its hands on their throats too.

And it was working.

Until he couldn't reach the other eyes. The construct had them not just on its arms and torso, but on its legs. There were three more, two of them just centimetres out of reach, one about an inch. He stretched, tipping the iris of one.

The armour around his neck buckled. He felt it dig into his neck, restricting the air flow. He gasped and wheezed. Time was running out quick now.

Then, just as his consciousness started to fade, he saw a little construct roll up beside them. Both Nox and the Iron Gunslinger looked at it, bemused. Then the creature plucked the cover off the Coilhunter's wrist pad. He hadn't the strength to fight it off. It was hopeless. Even the little ones were shedding his armour.

It pulled out a wire, which Nox thought it might try to strangle him with too. The Iron Gunslinger ignored it, as if it was nothing more than a fly. Right up until it shoved the wire into one of its open eye sockets, where it connected with the wires inside.

It sparked, and the Iron Gunslinger roared.

Its grip loosened, and then it hobbled back, striking the smaller construct and knocking it to the side. Nox yanked one of the metal platings around his neck free, then took a deep, gasping breath. He scrambled up, stumbling on the spot.

Then he watched the Iron Gunslinger charge at the little construct, and he knew they were not on the same side at all.

Chapter Thirty-five

TWO CONSTRUCTS
AND ONE WHEEL

The little construct pushed itself upright and spun around. It seemed almost to be taunting its much larger cousin. To dispel any doubt, it picked up a metal bar and tossed it at the Iron Gunslinger. That got its attention. The monstrous creature trudged after it, then halted to look back at the Coilhunter, who wavered on the spot. Then the little construct threw another object, and the Iron Gunslinger renewed its pursuit. You'd think Nox was the bigger threat, but right now he didn't feel like it.

He followed, slow and cautious. It wasn't like he could go quick. He could barely stand. Anyone else might have limped away. But Nox wasn't just curious. He had a feeling the little construct wasn't just playing cat and mouse.

They entered the area where the monowheel was, and the Coilhunter paused. The little construct gestured towards the vehicle, which was propped up with wires. The Iron Gunslinger stopped too, studying this new threat.

Nox didn't give it much time to study. He bashed the controls on his wristpad, firing up the engine. He knew there wasn't much fuel in it, so he had to act quick. He turned the wheel on, which scraped against the ground, jamming against some debris. It finally dislodged the junk, sending it flying behind, and the wheel spun madly, straining the wires.

The Iron Gunslinger had its arms out, ready to draw. But it had no guns.

The little construct snipped the wires with its pincers, and the monowheel sprang forward, darting across the ground and slamming into the Iron Gunslinger. It knocked the construct back, throwing it into one of the scrapyard walls. Debris tumbled down on it, pinning it in place.

Then the Coilhunter drove the monowheel back, realigned it, and climbed on board. He heard it creak beneath his weight. It was probably a good thing he'd lost some of his armour. He wasn't entirely sure how long it would hold, or how long the fuel would last.

He drove on, spotting Laura and Luke coming around the corner.

"Get on!" he shouted, skidding up beside them.

They clambered into the box on the back, barely getting one leg in before he drove off again.

Then they heard the sound of crashing steel. When they looked back, they saw the little construct zig-zagging after them, its tiny arms in the air. It had taken the time to paint a little O on its face, which they took for shock or fear.

Then the Iron Gunslinger stomped out, but it didn't come alone. The rubble that had tumbled down upon it contained other little constructs, which now clambered about its body, fusing themselves into all the cracks and crevices, giving it extra strength, and extra eyes. All of them settled on the monowheel. Now it had one target, but could kill all three of them.

It charged, crushing the earth beneath its now heavier feet, leaving giant prints behind. The ground shuddered as it moved, forcing the kids to hold on tighter. More scrap avalanched down on all sides, and some of it scurried after the Iron Gunslinger to fill in more of the gaps.

The monowheel stuttered and coughed. A dark smoke came out of the exhaust, like the one that came out of the Coilhunter's mask.

"We need fuel," he said.

Laura pulled the second canister from the side of the box.

"Where do I put it?"

Luke pointed to the oil-covered lid on the fuel tank. "In there, in there!" He grunted as he tried to unscrew it. The lid slipped out of his hands, but it was lucky he didn't slip out of the box with it. He tried to grab onto one of the metal bars running around the side, but his hands slipped. He shrieked as he tumbled forward, but Nox reached back, grabbing him by the shirt and pulling him back into place.

All the while, Laura tried to fill up the tank, but with all the bumps and tremors, she ended up pouring half the oil down the side instead. The little rolling construct skidded on some of the spillage, then dodged the rest, trying its best to keep up with them.

"Steady," she begged, but she probably should've prayed. Even then, she would've had to pray to the machine spirits, and right now it seemed they were animating every bit of scrap metal in the area.

"That's enough," Nox said, accelerating. "Throw the canister."

The girl launched it at the pursuing construct, as if it might somehow slow it down. Then, before it hit the ground, the remaining diesel sloshing around inside it, Nox turned back swiftly, stood up, and pulled a rifle from the side of the monowheel. He fired, and the bullet pierced the canister, causing a massive explosion just as the Iron Gunslinger ran into it. The force of the blast tore parts of it off, casting aside many of the smaller creatures that had assembled to repair it. It fell to one knee, then got back up, limping forward. Any surviving constructs crawled or rolled towards it.

"It's still comin'!" Luke screamed.

"Hang on," Nox said, barely giving them time to do it before he turned sharply. He headed towards one of the walls.

"What're you doing?" Laura cried.

"Trust me."

He could tell they closed their eyes. He almost did the same.

But just as they almost collided, and the Iron Gunslinger was almost upon them, he leant down hard to the right, enough for his entire seat to tilt with him, forcing the wheel to turn as sharply as ever. It pinged off the side of the wall, before blasting off again.

The Iron Gunslinger couldn't turn like that. Even with bits of it still hanging off, and other bits scrambling up its limbs, it trudged straight into the wall, causing the scrap to collapse down on top of it. It tried to struggle up and reached through the mess of things, but even its reaching arm was quickly buried by the seemingly endless fall of junk.

But like so much else in the Rust Valley, it was all interconnected. What fell there caused other things to fall elsewhere. Nox drove alongside the tumbling debris, which quickly formed a new wall, one much closer, yet almost as high as the last. He darted under the collapsing barriers, skidding past falling girders, narrowly missing engines that rolled like boulders down the metal mountains.

When it ended, Nox halted the monowheel, but not by choice. There was nowhere left to go. The tumbling scrap had sealed off all the passages on either side. The walls had moved, pinning them in a small clearing, while beyond those barriers the Rust Valley continued to conspire against them.

Chapter Thirty-six

A PRISON OF PIPE AND WIRE

Nox clambered off the monowheel, stumbled for a moment, then slumped to the ground. The kids jumped out after him and tried to help him up, but the best they could do was roll him around onto his back.

"I'm all right," he croaked, waving his hand dismissively.

"You don't look all right," Luke said.

"Why, shucks." Nox grunted as he pushed himself up onto one arm. "Better stick to your drawings, boy. Ya ain't got the manners for a nurse." He coughed, and felt blood splatter against the inside of his mask. He was glad the kids couldn't see it.

Luke might've frowned if he didn't have so much worry in his eyes. Nox barely realised the boy was clutching his arm tightly. Even wild little Aaron never did that—and he'd never do it now.

"You need to rest," Laura said, taking her neckerchief to wipe away some of the blood on the Coilhunter's forehead. It'd been rolling into his eyes, blocking his vision. He supposed that was the Iron Gunslinger's slow-release revenge. Nox didn't have any spares.

"We ain't got time for rest," Nox said. "They'll be back here."

"Well, you ain't any good dead," Laura said.

Luke shook his head while pouting. Nox never met a child who could pout as much as that boy. Words could do wonders, but there was nothing like a sullen face to play with your heartstrings.

"I'm not dead yet," Nox said, though he felt he was getting close. All these years, the sun'd tried to get him. It chased him daily across the desert, hounding him. Yet it was here in the darkness, while the sun was sleeping, that the grave started to open. Maybe the sun'd wonder why he didn't rise with it.

Nox tried to get up, much to Laura's protests, but he fell down just as quick, whacking his head off some of the scrap in the wall behind him. He groaned and rubbed his head.

"I told ya you need to rest," Laura said. Maybe that was how she was with Luke, when she thought he was having seizures. She might've thought they needed a mother, but as far as Nox could see, she was it. She had that instinct in her gut, just like he had the instinct to kill.

"Maybe just a minute," Nox said. He wanted to fight the urge to close his eyes. A lot could happen in a minute. Those constructs could be back. It took less than a minute to die.

"Luke," the girl said. "See if he's got medical supplies." She pointed to the monowheel.

"I do," Nox said, groggily, feeling his eyes shut like coffin lids before he pried them back open. It'd be easy to give in, to let it all go black. If it was just him, he might've even let it happen. But he heard Laura's voice, and saw Luke shuffling over to the monowheel, prodding at things to see if they'd open. He couldn't die just yet. He had to get them out.

"I'm not seein' any," Luke said. Through Nox's periodic glimpses, it looked like the boy was afraid to touch the vehicle after what'd happened last time.

"Front of the box," Nox said.

"There's nothin' there."

"Look harder!" Laura cried.

"I am!"

Laura got up and stomped over. "I'll find it."

Luke came back and knelt down beside Nox. "Will you be all right?"

"Maybe not all," Nox said, "but enough."

"What can I do?"

"Well, you can't see!" Laura shouted, coming back with the box of medical supplies. She pulled out a roll of bandages.

Luke stood up and kicked a stone away. It pinged off one of the walls, and he cringed at the sound. "Sorry."

"I need you to … find some weapons," Nox said.

"Weapons?"

"Guns, boy. Guns."

"But where?"

"It's the Wild North, boy," Nox said. "You'll find 'em everywhere."

Nox's consciousness faded quite a few times over the next hour or two. Between the long moments of blackness, he saw Laura dabbing his wounds and Luke wandering slowly around the edge of the clearing, pulling at the odd piece of metal.

Then, after watching a pile of old rifles form as if by magic nearby, he heard the boy shriek. Nox leapt up, forgetting his wounds. He raced over to Luke, where something in the debris had grabbed his arm. He wrapped his arms around the kid's waist to stop him from being pulled into the wall. Luke's cry echoed in the clearing. Nox summoned his strength and dragged Luke away, both of them falling to the ground. As he did, he pulled the construct free. It rolled forward.

"It's that one," Luke said, wiping away his tears.

That one was the little rolling creature that had helped Nox defeat the Iron Gunslinger. It spun on the spot and painted itself a little smile. The Coilhunter had asked Luke to find him some weapons. Some might've thought this more a toy. But Nox knew just how dangerous toys could be.

Chapter Thirty-seven

ODDCOPPER

At any other time, the Coilhunter would've gunned that little construct down. After what he'd seen, which was a lot worse than the terrors he'd heard of, every member of the Clockwork Commune had a Wanted poster in his mind. But this was different. This kind of proved the kids' mother right, that they weren't all bad. But then folk said that about the people of the Wild North. They didn't have to be *all* bad. Just enough of them had to be. That was when you didn't think twice with your trigger fingers.

"It's him," Luke said, brushing off the dust from his clothes.

"The thief," Laura added, placing her hands on her hips.

The construct hid its head inside its torso, peeping out periodically.

"I think it understands," Nox said.

"Mama said they do," Luke said. "Said they're like people."

Like people, Nox thought. That meant they were a mix of good and bad. You never quite knew what you were getting. But you could guess.

"Do you talk?" Nox asked the creature.

The construct's head rose again, slowly. It took its little paintbrush out and marked an X on its face where it should've had a mouth.

"I'll take that as a no."

"He keeps doin' that," Luke said. "Where does he get the paint?"

The construct pointed one stubby arm skyward.

"God?" Luke asked meekly, a little afraid to ask.

Nox scoffed mentally. That boy was still too young to realise that God had abandoned that place. But the Devil was still there, keeping everyone nice and warm.

The construct's body sank a little, which kind of looked like how it might make a sigh.

"Why, I'd say it means the balloons," Nox said. There wasn't much else in the sky worth noting—just that damn sun, watching all of them, and biding its sweet time. Just because it was hiding now didn't mean Nox forgot about it. Hell, that applied to the criminals too.

"The ones with the paintings?" Luke asked. Nox'd seen a drawing of an airship in the kid's journal, so he must've seen a different type travelling over the Wild North. Why it'd gone there was anyone's guess. Nox's guess was that it was madness.

"Doubt any other ones'd have paint for cargo."

The construct rose again. It bobbed its head up and down, which they took for a nod. When words wouldn't do, there was a universal language in gesture. You didn't need paint for that.

"Are you a boy or a girl?" Luke asked.

The construct seemed confused at first, until

Luke repeated the question, pointing at himself for boy and Laura for girl. It pointed at Luke.

"It's a boy."

"We got that," Laura said, rolling her eyes.

"Shut up," Luke replied, pouting.

"You got a name?" Nox asked the construct.

It stared at them blankly.

"I'm Luke," the boy said, pointing to himself. "This is my dumb sister, Laura."

The construct looked back and forth between them, confused.

"How 'bout we name you?" Luke suggested.

Laura scoffed and walked off.

"What d'ya think?" Luke asked Nox.

"I ain't much good with names."

"But you've got so many of 'em."

Nox chuckled, which sounded odd in his mask. "I don't pick those myself."

Luke pondered for a moment, rubbing his chin dramatically. "Come to think of it, I didn't pick mine either. So … it's a tradition then. We gotta name him."

"Well, go ahead, boy," Nox said. "I'm better at crossin' names off lists."

Luke took out his journal again and started writing down names, most of which sounded better for a pet. He had a dog back at the ranch, old Banjo. He still had a drawing of him in his journal. That was all he had. He died when the bandits attacked.

After a time, where the Coilhunter sorted through the rifles, Luke settled on a name.

"Oddcopper," he proclaimed. "That it! I got it. I got your name."

The construct painted a little smile on its face, but Nox wasn't sure if that was more out of politeness than anything else. It begged the question: just how close to people were these things? He knew the original ones were made by some mad professor from Blackout, but he'd heard too many different versions of the story. And maybe that was all it was. A story. At one time, he thought that was all the Clockwork Commune were too. You soon learned to pay heed to fables in the Wild North. Some of them turned out to be true.

But truth or lie, it was good to see Luke's cheerfulness. It might've been one of the few times he'd etched out a little joy for himself from this whole affair. And that was the thing about joy. You had to dig for it like gold—and like gold, you might never find it. But iron? There was plenty of that. It was what made the wheels of industry and war go round. The Iron Empire had people digging for that too.

As Luke interacted with Oddcopper, he reminded Nox of a mix of his own kids: of the compassion Ambrose had for others, and of the curiousness of Aaron. But then Nox thought maybe he was searching for things that weren't really there, like gold—or like ghosts. He glanced at Laura, who sat glaring from the edge of the clearing, full of the hidden anger that Luke didn't really try to hide. Sometimes the children left the parents, and sometimes the parents left the children. Nox tried to imagine what it was like for them, being abandoned for research, for science—for constructs just like this one.

Nox knew it wasn't healthy to make comparisons,

but folk had a love of doing unhealthy things. Ambrose and Aaron. Laura and Luke. It was tradition in the Wild North to name your kids with the same letter if you wanted them to get on. Came from the tribes, people said. Nox went along with it once, but he scoffed at it now. *More like superstition.* The names didn't stop them from fighting. And no charms or rituals stopped them from dying. They just made living a little easier.

Luke cried out suddenly, and Nox leapt up, guns at the ready. It was lucky he wasn't a "shoot first" kind of guy or it might've ended bad. Turned out it was just Luke's excitement as Oddcopper dug Nox's guide owl from the debris.

"Hell, boy," Nox said, "don't scream like that."

"Sorry. It's just … look. The bird with the big eyes."

"You mean the owl?"

"Is that what you call it?"

"It's what everyone calls it. You never seen an owl before?"

It was a stupid question. This kid was born too close to the time of the Harvest, when the Iron Empire came. A lot of kids of that time hadn't seen a lot of things. Except dust. They saw plenty of that. And crime. And war. The Wild North might've been left as "neutral territory," but it was just as affected as the rest. There was always desert—but it didn't always reach so far.

"I saw an eagle once," Luke said, looking away wistfully. "At least, I think it was one. Papa said it was just a hawk. But it was bigger. We went out to find it, but it was gone."

He pulled out his journal and flicked through the pages until he found a drawing of a bird perched on a cactus.

"I drew it before it flew off."

"Well, looks like you've got an eagle eye, boy. That's an eagle all right."

"Is it? How d'you know?"

"It's a predator. I know my predators."

"Oh."

The boy started to close his journal, but Nox spotted something on one of the newer pages.

"Go back," he said. "What's that?"

The boy blushed. "Oh, it's not ready yet." He showed a half-finished drawing of the Coilhunter, which he must've made when Nox was sleeping.

"Quite a likeness," Nox said.

In fact, it was too much of a likeness. It showed his dark eyes, the crags in his skin, and that damn mask. It was like one of those captured images produced in the dark chambers that folk were going crazy for of late. Old Five-pence Tully had a darkroom wagon hauled by mules, which she toured the width and breadth of Altadas in, capturing moments for a bit more than five pence now. Some still did the calculations from the old currency to coils, but Nox didn't bother. The Treasury thought you could rely on money. They were wrong. But guns? Well, you could rely on them no problem.

"I still need to work on it," Luke said, putting his journal away. "Maybe I'll draw Oddcopper next." He tapped his foot off the construct's hull. "Would ya like that, huh?"

The day wore on, and Nox felt his strength returning, though more from necessity than anything else. He repaired the owl and shoved it back into his shoulder pad. His armour creaked. He thought some of it was a little beyond repair. He might as well've been wearing one of those buckled hulls that lined the scrap heaps.

But there wasn't too much time for mending. He could hear the minutes counting down in his head. Hell, he could hear them in the ticks inside Oddcopper's body, barely muted by the metal plating. There was one thing you could really count on. Time wasn't on your side. Like everything else in the Wild North, it was out to get you.

Laura pulled Luke aside, as far away from Oddcopper as she could get him, which took some trying, as the construct kept following them around.

"Should we be trustin' this thing?" Laura asked.

Luke shuffled on the spot. "Why not?"

"They're to blame for all this. They're why mama and papa came out here."

"Yeah, but that doesn't mean they're bad."

"You saw what the other ones did."

"The other ones, yeah. But not this one."

"But can we trust it?" Laura asked.

The Coilhunter walked past, halting. "You trust your gut," he said, before throwing a rifle her way. "Or you trust this."

Chapter *Thirty-eight*

GUN-SHY

"Here, boy," Nox said, throwing a rifle his way. To the Coilhunter's surprise, Luke flinched, stepping back and raising his clenched fists. The gun struck the ground.

"What's the matter?" Nox asked. He knew it wasn't just a case of a boy who couldn't catch. That boy didn't want to catch. That boy didn't want to shoot.

"I don't like guns," Luke said.

"Most don't, but you get to like 'em."

"I don't wanna."

"Well, boy, you either get to like guns, or other people's guns get to like you."

"I know, but—"

"He's always like this," Laura said.

"I ain't a yellow-belly," the boy said.

Nox shifted his feet. "Didn't say you were."

"But people think it."

"Well, people think a lot of things. Ain't no point worryin' about what's goin' on in their heads. It's the world out here that we've got to worry about."

"I don't wanna be another killer."

"Didn't your father teach ya to shoot?"

"He tried," Laura said. "By gosh, he tried. Luke just wanted to draw."

Nox humphed. "Well, I can teach ya to draw another way. But it ain't any good if you ain't willin' to pull the trigger."

"I'll do it," Laura said, cocking her rifle.

"I know *you* will, but we're outnumbered bad here. We got six hands between us, not countin' whatever you call those clamps on Oddcopper. We can't afford to have any hands not holdin' a weapon."

Luke's eyes were already watering. Normally kids his age were eager to shoot, more eager than did them any good. Nox didn't want to force him, but he didn't want him to die either. If you didn't want to die in the Wild North, you learned pretty quick to pick up a pistol. Luke was lucky he had Laura or he'd have probably already learned that lesson the hard way.

Then, with all eyes on the boy, Luke crouched down and picked the rifle up gingerly, holding it away from him, like you might a snake.

"You know how to shoot it?" Nox asked.

"You pull the trigger."

"Yeah, well that's the gist of it."

Luke chewed his lip. "What if I kill someone?"

"Well, that's the point."

"But I don't wanna do that."

"You're lucky we're in the Rust Valley, then, boy. It's mostly just us."

"But the constructs," Luke said.

"What about 'em?"

"Isn't that killin' too?"

"Not sure ya can kill what ain't alive, but I ain't no

philosopher."

Luke looked at Oddcopper, who peered back with curious eyes. "But aren't they alive?"

His mother could've probably answered that. Hell, it was her questions that started this whole mess in the first place. It was simpler with men. Most were so rotten, you could almost smell the stench. You didn't think twice about killing those.

"In their own way, maybe," Nox said.

"They're just machines," Laura said.

"But mama—"

"Mama left us."

"But—"

"Ain't we life too, Luke?"

They caught each other's glances.

"She left us to die, Luke. We could've died."

Nox couldn't help the thought: *You might still.*

"I don't know if this takes the sting out," Nox said, "but you ain't the only one who'd rather hold a pencil than a pistol. Ever heard of Rommond?" That war hero from the Resistance side had a way of taking the sting out for many, and putting it back in for the rest.

"The general?" Luke asked, wiping one eye with the back of his hand. The rifle wavered in his grip. The boy'd have to lose those shudders or he might kill someone all right—and not the right one.

"The very same," Nox said. "Well, last I heard, he'd rather be at home paintin'. Quite a dab hand at it too, or so I hear. But the war's on down south, the Great Iron War, and he ain't got a home. He's just got a battlefield, and a cause. Hell, he ain't got a choice."

Luke dug the heel of his foot into the ground,

rocking it from side to side. "He could say no."

"Then he'd be consignin' hundreds, hell probably thousands, to die."

"But he's a soldier."

"He's more than a soldier, boy. We all are."

"But don't it give you nightmares?"

Nox was glad the kid couldn't see his eyes. *Yeah*, he thought. *It gives ya terrible ones. But so does everything here. So does not fightin'.*

"You already have those," Laura said, saving Nox from having to reply.

"But I don't want worse ones."

"Don't be afraid of it, boy," Nox said. "A gun ain't nothin' but a hunk o' metal."

"But we ain't nothin' but flesh and bone."

Nox smiled. "I think we're a little more than that. Why, I'd say those drawings of yours proves that just fine."

Chapter Thirty-nine

GOIN' OVER THE TOP

They climbed up the scrapyard wall, slow and steady. There were many footholds, but many more places to lose your footing. The wall shifted and shook as they went, and they were never entirely certain that a mechanical arm wouldn't reach out from it to grab them—or push them off.

When they reached the summit, and glanced back down at Oddcopper, who circled the clearing sullenly, they got a bird's eye view of much of the Rust Valley. It was quite a sight. Those winding walls went on for what looked like miles. Some said the Clockwork Commune had made themselves a town from the junk. They'd done more than that. They'd made a sprawling city. Hell, Nox might've even called it an empire. But there was only one Iron Empire in Altadas. Someone had to go. Nox wasn't entirely sure who it'd be.

"You still hell-bent on searchin' all that?" Nox asked Laura.

"You would," she replied, "if it was your mama."

"I suppose I would."

"But," Laura said, "maybe we won't find her."

"Sometimes you don't." Nox had spent many years

in searches of his own, to the point that he'd almost given up. Yet even then, a part of him pushed him on. It was the same part that urged him to survive. Some people lived to live, but he lived for vengeance. Even now, with vengeance had, that part of him wanted more. *You'll never be satisfied*, he thought to himself, a message for Laura, and a message for himself.

Then his eyes caught the glint of something far off. From the wall tops, he could see Porridge's copter, still parked, only a few scrapyard streets away. He only hoped that Porridge had that urge to survive as strong as he did.

"We're close to gettin' outta here," Nox said, pointing to the copter.

"What is it?" Luke asked. From this far off, it looked like a heap of junk, almost blending into the background. Up close, it didn't look a whole lot better.

Laura perked up. "Could that be—?"

"No," Nox said, knowing what she meant. *It ain't your mama. God knows where she is. Why, maybe he don't know either.* He was thankful for the privacy of thoughts. You got to voice the ugly truth without ever forcing good folk to hear it. But bad folk? Well, he'd have no problem forcing them.

"It's a friend," Nox added. "And a way out. We just need to get there."

"We need to get down first," Luke said, peering down the steep slope. "It's dark down there."

It was. It was like the shadows had gathered around the iron prison. Who knew what hid inside them.

"Well then," Nox said. "Ain't it lucky I brought the

174

light."

He struck his shoulder pad, which fired the newly-restored mechanical owl out into the sky. It hovered above the cloud of darkness for a moment, flapping its wings. Then its eyes lit up, revealing a horde of constructs assembled below.

While Luke and Laura gasped at the sight, the Coilhunter leapt into action. He threw himself off the edge, firing a grappling hook towards the owl. It latched on, and he swung across the area, firing a rifle with his other hand. He barely even needed to aim. Everywhere below, he had a shot.

Then, as he cleared a little opening in the centre of the horde, and as the owl struggled to support his weight, he snapped the wire and landed with a thud amidst the ravenous constructs. They turned to him and raised their blades and saws and bits of rusted metal. He turned to them and raised his guns.

He fired, just as the first of them leapt at him, letting his metal-piercing bullets tear through their mechanical innards, breaking the chains of cogs and springs, strewing apart their assembled hearts. He didn't wait for them to stumble or fall. He turned his rifles on the next, like the hands of a steady clock, even as he ended the ticks and tocks of the leaping constructs around him. Everything was the bang of guns and the clash of metal. Nox threw aside the emptied rifles, not even bothering to reload them. He just pulled another pre-loaded one from his back, and then two at a time. He was just as sure a shot with both hands. But like a clock, he only had two hands, and he couldn't point at every number. As some went down in front of him, others leapt up behind him, stabbing and slashing at the nape of his neck. There was armour there, but he wasn't the only one with armour-piercing weapons. Some of them had saws built into their arms which could slice through plating as if it were butter.

That was when Laura's practised shots came in. She didn't go all guns blazing like Nox did. She couldn't. She only had one gun. Instead, she took it slow and steady, lining up each shot, holding it in her line of sight until she was certain she had the kill. That was how she did it back at the ranch when the bandits came. That was how half of those bandits wound up dead. If she hadn't run out of bullets, she might've got the rest of them too.

So, now she didn't waste a shot. Just as a saw clipped the Coilhunter's armour, she blasted that construct apart, careful not to pierce Nox instead. Luke tried to follow suit, eyeing up a shot for a long time like Laura, but he never pulled the trigger. If you were facing bandits, that might've been all you needed. A deterrent. But the constructs didn't fear bullets like men did. They craved the metal, even if it left them dead.

By the end of it, which came swifter for the constructs than even the Coilhunter expected, the ground was more cluttered than ever. Sometimes you couldn't even tell those heaps of scrap were once living things—or if maybe they were still living. It was a lot cleaner than Nox's usual gunfights. The ground was littered with oil and cogs instead of blood and guts.

The kids climbed down as quick as they could,

with Laura taking more care, and Luke jumping off about five feet from the bottom. The boy dusted himself off and checked that he still had his satchel. Normally in the Rust Valley you had to check if you still had your legs. There was time for that yet.

"We've gotta be quick," Nox said. They were so close to the copter, but the winding passages meant they had to travel farther away before they could get there. Sometimes to get to safety you had to move closer to danger.

"What about Oddcopper?" Luke asked. "He can't climb."

"We have to leave him."

"Why?"

"He can't climb."

"But they'll kill him."

"They'll kill us."

It hadn't quite dawned on Nox that Laura was awfully quiet. She hadn't condemned the little rolling construct. She hadn't urged them on or offered to fight the good fight. Instead, her face grew slowly ashen, and her eyes grew wide. When Nox finally noticed it, he turned to see where she was staring.

There, in the distance, half covered in shadow, was a woman, surrounded by many different constructs of all shapes and sizes. She didn't look like a prisoner. She didn't look like prey.

Luke gasped when he saw her.

"Mama."

MAMA

You could tell she was their mama. She had their same thick, sun-bleached hair. She had that same roundness in her face. She even had that same look of sorrow in her deep blue eyes. She was their mama all right. But the Coilhunter knew that right now, she was also something else.

Luke tried to run to her, letting himself be reeled in by the heart. But Nox held out his arm, blocking the kid's advance. The boy looked up at him, but Nox kept his eyes on the woman across the way, that woman surrounded by so many constructs that it almost looked like she had joined the Commune. They say looks can be deceiving, but sometimes things are just what they seem.

"Luke!" the woman cried, clutching the sides of her dress. "Laura!"

Nox could feel Luke trying to press forward, so he pressed back. Laura didn't try at all. Though she'd came looking for her mama, she'd likely found it wasn't to come running into her arms. It was so she could tell her face to face what she felt deep inside. It wasn't wisdom that held her back. It was anger.

"Wait," Nox said quietly, as Luke struggled with

his arm. The boy would have dug his nails in if the Coilhunter wasn't wearing armour. Right now, Nox was thinking that maybe they all needed shields.

"Where were you?" Laura shouted across. The distance between them was just far enough to play a game of fifty paces. There was no brush between, no rolling tumbleweeds. Just those two opposing forces, ready to sling their tongues.

"I was here," her mother said, stating the obvious. Nox knew what Laura really meant: *why did you go?* She'd heard the first answer her mother gave all those months ago, that tale about research and science. That explained where she was going. It didn't explain why she left.

"You left us," Laura said. Nox could hear the anger in her voice, tempered by tears. The Wild North would dry those up soon enough, leaving just the anger. It did it to the best of them. The worst of them already came dried up.

"I had to find out." Her mother seemed quite earnest, almost pleading as she spoke. She didn't have to say it with her words. She said it with her eyes. *Please believe me.*

"Well?" Nox asked. "What did ya find?" He let the grit gather in his throat, where there were none of his own tears clogging the way. He let his voice rattle off like gunfire. He let the black smoke explode out of his mask, as if his whole body was now a smoking gun.

The mother looked at him, with her own questions in her eyes. She no doubt wondered who he was. He had an answer for that. *I'm the one who*

179

picked up the pieces after you left. The Wild North was full of broken families, but most mothers who were gone didn't leave willingly. They left at the end of the barrel of a gun. But her? She had a choice.

"What did you find?" Laura asked. If she wouldn't answer the Coilhunter, she'd have to answer her.

"They're just like us," her mother said.

Nox humphed. "You mean they abandon their young?"

The woman had too many tears in her eyes to give him a fiery glare. He might've even pitied her, were it not for his gut reminding him where they were, and for his eyes reminding him of all those constructs surrounding her, not moving an inch, not flaying the skin off her like they did to everyone else.

"I *had* to know," she said. People in the Wild North weren't known for their conviction. The criminals flipped from one gang to another, offing the leader to gain favour in the next, until they ended up in the way of someone else. The rest of the folk paid protection money to any gang that came their way, until they eventually ended up paying both sides. There wasn't room for conviction there, just like there wasn't room for law. But Nox'd make room.

"So?" Nox asked. "Did you find that key to perpetual motion?"

"No," she replied. "I found somethin' better."

"What'd you find?"

"I found out how to merge metal and flesh."

Then something advanced from the shadows behind her, and Nox was quick to pull out a gun. But he didn't fire. It wasn't quite the shock that held him back, or the fact that he saw a man there, with parts of him replaced with machinery. It was what Luke said.

"Papa."

Chapter Forty-one

PAPA

Luke didn't try to run to his father. Only part of that creature standing across the way was his papa. The other part—or the other parts—were something else. They weren't just scrapyard metal. They were as living as he was. He was a collection of pieces, as good as any other member of the Clockwork Commune.

"What did you do?" Laura asked, struggling with the words.

"I made a miracle," her mother said.

An abomination, Nox thought. He would've said it out loud, but wanted to save the kids from hearing it. He would've liked to save them from seeing it too.

Their papa's left arm was entirely replaced from the shoulder down, ending in a three-finger clamp. His jaw was iron, and part of his ribcage was ripped out, with metal plating soldered straight into the skin. His right foot was gone, ending in a piece of iron girder. Clearly he was a work in progress. Maybe there'd be nothing of him left by the time she was done.

"You're a monster," Luke blurted. Maybe he also only meant to think it. Or maybe he meant those words for his mama. You could have all your human parts and still be one.

"Don't say that, Luke," his papa said. A tear rolled down his cheek, straight onto his iron jaw. Maybe there was still a human heart in him after all.

"This is our next step," his mama said. "Our evolution."

"I thought evolution was what happened in nature," Nox said. "Ain't nothin' natural about this."

"We made them," she replied. "Years ago now. Doctor Ailswee Barnaby. A brilliant man." She kind of twitched as she spoke, but there weren't any cogs or pistons moving her. "But now it's come full circle. They can make us. Life making life, making life."

Nox didn't know about that. He knew about death much better. Didn't matter if you were made of metal or flesh. It came for you just as good. Maybe, in that way, there wasn't much of a difference. But right now he could see a difference. He could see she was crazy.

"We were gonna come back," she said, looking to her kids now, clenching her hands together as if it were a long-held prayer. "We'd come back. We wouldn't just keep this gift to ourselves. We'd share it with you too."

Nox's fingers clenched his gun a little tighter. Her words were like someone else drawing a gun. It was one thing them making monsters of themselves, but her eyes were on Luke and Laura now. Nox swore silently to himself that her hands wouldn't be on them too.

"You're crazy," Nox said.

"That's what they said about all advances in science. Don't you think people look at you and your gadgets and your monowheel, and don't you think they think you're crazy too?"

And maybe they did, and maybe she thought that she was just making the world a better place, just like him. But she'd already hurt her kids. He wasn't going to let her do it again.

The father was silent, the obedient lapdog. There were enough of those at the sides of the mad and the menacing, helping them achieve their evil end. You didn't have to be the one who pulled the trigger. You just had to be silent while it was happening. Silence was an inexhaustible ammunition, held by good people too.

Nox saw Luke looking over at Laura, a desperate plea for what to do. Maybe he wanted her to tell him that it was okay, that those two monsters across the way were still their parents, that they could all go back to playing happy family. But it'd just be playing. That boy had learnt well the damage that lies could do.

"Won't you come with us?" his mama asked. She must've noticed his glance to his sister, spotted that little moment of doubt, and leapt on it like a predator. She was so quick to ditch her kids, and just as quick to scoop them back up. They'd be just another set of bodies in her experiments.

"They ain't goin' nowhere," Nox said, placing a firm hand on Luke's shoulder, keeping the other clutching his gun.

Their mama didn't look at him. She bypassed him entirely, setting her pleading, preying eyes on her little boy and girl, looking back and forth between them.

She played their hearts like Nox played his guitar. You could almost hear the twang.

But Luke and Laura replied with a silence of a different kind. It wasn't the silence of obedience or acquiescence, or of looking the other way. It was the silence of defiance, even if it was so terribly hard to defy.

The constructs took a small, almost imperceptible step forward. Nox saw it, making a small, almost imperceptible adjustment to his gun. Mama and papa weren't going to take no for an answer. They were going to have their family back, or they were going to discipline them.

"Back off," Nox said. "Don't let this get ugly. Don't you think they've seen enough?"

"We want them to see the way. This is the only way."

Nox knew that wasn't true. He raised the pistol. "I know another."

The glares were intense. The tears were gone in their mama's eyes. Now there was just the fire, like the periodic flames that dotted the ruins of the Rust Valley. Their papa stared blankly, like an empty vessel. Yet when the constructs took a step forward, he did too.

Nox kept his eyes on them, and kept his gun on them too. He took a deep breath, letting the smoke filter out slowly. He spoke the next words slow and quiet, just high enough for the kids to hear them.

"Run."

Chapter Forty-two

RUN

The children ran, but so did the constructs that surrounded their parents. They leapt out in force and number, too many for the Coilhunter's bullets. He gunned them down, not one by one, but in twos and threes, until bullet casings clattered off the ground as quickly as his scrapyard foes. He backed away with each blast, stealing another second, giving them all to the trigger.

And then, far behind, where he could barely hear the frantic footfalls of Luke and Laura, he heard a mighty crash. He turned his head just enough to see, keeping his guns pointed forward. His eyes went wide at the sight of the scrapyard wall they had previously been imprisoned in bursting apart. Out of the debris came the Iron Gunslinger, more patchwork than ever, with new eyes that settled on the panicked children that stood in shock before it.

So Nox ran too. Not away from danger, but straight into it. He ran for the children, and for this undying foe, knowing well that he could not replace his own limbs or eyes, and did not bleed oil. But then neither could Luke or Laura, so long as Nox kept them away from their parents' experiments.

One of the Iron Gunslinger's legs was pinned inside the wall, but it was tall and vast, and could swipe with its mighty arms. Debris still rained down from its entrance, but for every piece that landed, it threw another up into the air, launching flattened vehicles towards the Coilhunter as it raced across. Nox dodged one, then rolled out of the way of another, with the weight of his armour almost toppling him as he got back to his feet. He stumbled on, grimacing as a landship turret struck his leg, then grunting as he tripped over a tyre that skidded towards his feet.

Then the rain of debris stopped, and he watched as the Iron Gunslinger scooped up Laura in one mighty fist and shoved her into an opening in the scrap wall, sealing the entrance with the hull of a burnt-out truck. As Luke tried to stop it and free his sister, it snatched him up. The boy shouted and flailed and squirmed, but the hands grew tighter around his waist. Nox skidded to a halt, pulling his rifle from his back. This was it, he knew. The last gun. The last shots. He could almost hear the last, fleeting breaths of Luke to match.

He aimed at the claws clutching Luke, but he knew he didn't quite have the shot just yet. Even then, he could hear the scurrying and ticking of the horde of constructs behind him. The Iron Gunslinger barely moved, but Luke kept on struggling, forcing the construct to adjust position.

Hold steady, boy, Nox thought. He meant it also for his gun.

Then he felt the constructs grab him, and he tensed his arms to keep the gun in place. They leapt upon him and each other, scrambling up each other's backs, crawling between the cracks of their kin, until he was almost buried beneath them. Just his head and gun popped through.

He waited, even as he drowned beneath the metal, until he found that perfect shot. He fired, and the armour-piercing bullet cleaved through one of the Iron Gunslinger's fingers. Luke dropped to the ground, landing on his back with a thud. Nox barely had time to see the boy twist and turn in place before his sight was blocked entirely. Even the rifle was washed away by the iron tide and left on some distant scrapyard shore.

Nox didn't bother with prayers, even though he now had the empty hands for them. He wouldn't know who to pray to, and he damn well knew no one was answering. Not here. The Wild North was its own kind of limbo. For some, it was Heaven. For most, it was Hell. Nox knew this moment would come sooner or later. He'd been lucky to put it off for so long. You got your ration of luck like you got your ration of water, but unlike the latter, you couldn't pay for more. For most, it pretty quickly ran out. Nox felt he'd probably had a few drops more than he should've, but then so did some criminals. And maybe that was how you got more—by taking it from someone else.

But just when all seemed lost, the darkness broke, and he saw gaps forming again in his cage of metal. The constructs clambered off him. For a moment, he thought they were letting him go. Then he felt their tight pincers clamping his wrists and ankles, holding him in place. They weren't going anywhere. They were just letting someone else get a better view.

The kids' mama approached, but right now there was nothing motherly about her. She stood right over him, writing his name in her notebook. He didn't know hers, but he knew she was Mrs. Mayfield. That was enough for a poster, enough for a prize. When she was done with his name, which she recorded as Nathaniel Osley Xander, she crossed off some items from a list, then tucked the notepad back into her belt. She was done with the name, but she wasn't done with him. He could see sketches of human-machine hybrids on the first page. Now he knew where Luke'd got it from. He hoped he hadn't inherited anything else.

Mrs. Mayfield didn't even smile. "Open him up," she said, with that same kind of deadpan tone. After all, she was doing this for science. There was no room for emotion. Only logic. Nox didn't see much of that himself. Only madness.

A construct hobbled over, with a large rotating saw for an arm. Two other constructs held it in place before the saw started spinning. Nox squinted as the sparks flew in all directions. He took a deep puff of that numbing mix of oxygen and chemicals in his tank, his own kind of hybrid.

Then Mrs. Mayfield made her first smile. "Let's see what makes him tick."

Chapter Forty-three

MAKING MONSTERS

The saw struck the armour, slicing it in two. Nox struggled with his bonds, but the constructs held him tight. He couldn't reach any of the gadgets on his belt, and he didn't have many left there to begin with. They'd soon add those to their mechanical bodies, and his to the scrap heap.

And then they stopped. The saw didn't go through his flesh, like he expected, and like how the Clockwork Commune had operated to date. They had a new ruler, or perhaps this group was just one of many factions, like the dozens of gangs that made the Wild North their home. These constructs didn't dig through flesh in search of metal. They wanted to merge the two.

So, they stripped him of his armour, taking it off plate by plate. There was a lot to remove, so it took some time, and in the process of it all, where Nox vacillated between utter resignation and a periodic determination to form a plan of escape, he spotted Luke scurrying behind the rubble far away. He also saw the Iron Gunslinger, now frozen, as if it didn't entirely operate of its own accord. Laura's sobs were audible from the makeshift cage she sat inside.

Mrs. Mayfield must've noticed his stares. "Don't worry about her," she said, pointing to the massive construct. "I made that." She said the rest with her eyes: *I made it for you.*

Nox spoke through gritted teeth. "Monsters making monsters."

"In the world of the bounty hunter, everything's conveniently so black and white. You don't see the grey, or the myriad of other colours, all mixing together, becoming better for it, becoming indefinable."

"I know evil when I see it."

"But you don't know good."

The last piece of armour was removed, but they left him with his mask and oxygen tank. Mrs. Mayfield ran her fingers across it, then down the pipes to the back.

"You're halfway there already, Coilhunter."

"And so are you," he said, forcing the thick black smoke into her face. "Halfway to Hell."

"You and your religion."

"You and your science. Let's meet halfway and just call it all madness."

"It's what you do with it," she said.

"Exactly. And you ain't doin' nothin' good."

"The families of those you kill for money might say somethin' similar."

He was no construct, but she was pushing his buttons now. Many had tried that, but he pushed back.

"You're one to talk about families," he said. He knew that was one of her buttons. He could see the reaction in her eyes. If you had a soul—and some acted like they didn't—you had to contend with a little niggling thing called guilt. You could push it down like you pushed other people's buttons. You could bury it beneath the scrapyard of the soul. But just like the hidden things beneath the debris of the Rust Valley, sooner or later it came out.

So Mrs. Mayfield stopped pushing buttons. Instead, she pulled off his mask, exposing the scars, and exposing his lungs to the cool night air. He tried to hold his breath, but his lungs were too badly damaged to hold it for long.

"We could fix this," she said, running her fingers across his scars. They didn't hurt now—not the physical ones. She moved her hand down his chest, pressing against his ribcage. He felt the tenderness there, even now. "We could fix all of it."

There were quack doctors throughout Altadas who'd said the same. Some showed him their iron lungs. Some went with copper instead. He even met a young man who'd had the operation. He didn't live long. And when those quacks turned up on the Wanted posters, well, they didn't live long either.

"A mechanic like you'd be useful," Mrs. Mayfield said.

There it was: the price. He was on her own Wanted poster. All it'd cost was his soul. It didn't have the words "Dead or Alive." As a hybrid, you didn't get a choice. You'd be both.

"I'll never join your army," Nox spat. He got to spit it now, without his mask. He couldn't use those menacing puffs of smoke instead.

"You don't have to. We'll take out those parts of

your brain that make you say no."

"You should probably use a bullet for that," he replied, taking a painful gasp at the end. "That's the only thing that'll work on me."

Or this, Nox thought. *Just leave the mask off long enough.*

"We'll see about that," Mrs. Mayfield said, putting the mask back and standing up. "We'll see soon enough."

But their sight was suddenly drawn by something else. The battered hull of a landship slid down from the mountain of scrap nearby, bringing an avalanche of other mangled parts. And with that movement, there was something else.

Oddcopper.

The little rolling construct scurried through the debris, making straight for the fallen rifle. Nox was never so happy in his life to see a construct. He silently rooted it on, calling out its name in his mind. Laura wasn't silent at all. She yelled the name through her iron bars.

"Oddcopper! Go! Go!"

And it went, zooming past flying debris, dodging leaping constructs. It seemed like no matter what they threw at it, nothing hit.

And then Nox thought he saw it start to slow.

No, he thought. He couldn't even shake his head.

Oddcopper approached the weapon and reached down, but its body locked into place, with one arm outstretched towards the gun. And it froze. The little wind-up heart inside it ran out of beats, and its ticking, which had been slowing for days, ceased entirely. Its little eyes went dark. So too did everyone's hope.

And then Luke raced out from his cover. He grabbed the rifle, struggling to hold it up. He pointed it at his mother, who turned in amazement to see her gun-shy son before her.

"Put that down, Luke."

"No," he said, not much more than a whisper.

"Put it down."

"No!" he shouted, like the bang of bullet fire.

"You'll hurt someone," his mother said, holding her hands out. She almost seemed calm and gentle, almost like a mother. She stepped forward.

"That's the point," Nox said, drawing her attention his way. He saw she was getting a little too close. People had done that in his early days too, and he'd learned the hard way. You never let them close the gap. If they tried, they died.

As she turned back to Luke, Nox gave the slightest of gestures to the boy to move back. That kid wasn't just inexperienced—he had no experience at all. You couldn't draw yourself out of this fight. He had to replace the lead pencil with just lead.

Luke stepped back, glancing down at his feet as he did. It was easy to see why, with all the debris around. He could've backed into anything. That was why you studied your terrain first. Then you spent the rest of the time studying your foe. You didn't look away in the showdown or more than likely you'd go down first.

But Mrs. Mayfield didn't want to kill Luke. Deep beneath the monster was a mother. By the looks of it, very deep. If nothing else, the boy was a specimen, young and healthy, just like Coilcountin' Lawson saw him. An asset. Who knew how the hybrid process would take to his developing organs. There was only one way to know for sure.

"Step back!" Luke yelled, nudging the rifle towards her.

She halted, but she didn't step back.

"Son," she said, soft and gentle. How she must've said that at night when she tucked him in. How she must've said it with a kiss as morning came.

"You're not my mama," he said, though it didn't sound like he wholly believed it. His brow was furrowed, and his features shifted between a grimace and a pout.

"Don't say that."

"Don't be this," he whimpered.

"I'm still your mama." Maybe she meant it as a form of comfort, but Nox couldn't help but hear it as: *Put that down, boy. I can still give you a whoopin'.* But the Coilhunter had his own thought: *So can he.*

"You left us," Luke said, his voice soft again. No doubt he wanted an explanation. He'd already gotten an answer to that, but it wasn't good enough. *She* wasn't good enough.

"I only went—"

"You left us," he said again, a little louder.

"It was only—"

"You left us!" Laura screamed from her iron prison. If only leaving were the worst of their mother's crimes.

Their father stepped forward, with a clang in his

step. "It was for a good cause," he said. Maybe he even believed it. Or maybe he always just operated like a machine, responding to his wife's every beck and call.

"A good cause," his mama repeated, like a mantra. She wrung her hands together as if she really hoped he believed her, or maybe she just hoped she'd believe herself.

Luke shook his head. "It don't look good, mama."

"Things don't always look the way they are."

Luke snuffled. "Then it's lies, mama."

"Don't you talk to your mama like that," his papa said. He raised an admonitory finger, but it was made of metal.

Luke turned the gun on him. "You left us too."

"I had to," he said. Just like clockwork.

"We had to fight," Luke said, looking at the rifle like he'd looked at the one he held when the bandits came. "You weren't there. The raiders came and you weren't there. I kept drawin' you, both of you, in my pictures, 'cause you weren't there!"

"We're here now, love," his mama said.

He pointed the gun back to her.

"We're here now."

Don't let 'em fool ya, Nox thought. He urged the boy on with his eyes. He didn't want him to shoot, but he didn't want him to not shoot either. He just wanted him to get out of there, alive. He couldn't do that if he gave in that gun.

"Let him go, mama," Laura shouted over. She had one arm hanging down through a gap in the cage. "Let them both go. You can have me instead."

"No," Nox said. "Let the kids go. I'm more useful

to you."

"But I already have you," Mrs. Mayfield said, and then she looked at Laura. "I already have the both o' you."

Luke looked at them, and then to his mother. Nox could see the thoughts in his eyes. He was thinking of offering the same. *No*, Nox thought, shaking his head gently. *No, Luke. Don't give in. You're the only one of us with a gun.*

"Hand the weapon over," his papa urged. Back in the towns, folk used to call him Wholesome Hank. He was that full of good morals, a true upstanding citizen, an obeyer of the law, even when there wasn't any law to obey. Luke had heard his mother call his papa that in jest, and he'd watched from the bannisters as she tickled Hank's chin, and as he grabbed her up and kissed her neck.

"Hand the weapon over," his papa repeated, looking at him with one wholesome eye, and one that was made of machinery.

Don't do it, Nox said with his own.

"Hand it over, son."

But little Luke, who never had a nickname, who never fired a weapon, didn't hand it over.

"You ain't got it in you to shoot," his papa said.

Little Luke, little Gun-shy Luke, who the Mayfields thought they knew so well, little Lead-chewin' Luke, who'd spent so long looking down at his journal. He cocked the rifle. The sound echoed through the Rust Valley.

"I don't wanna shoot you," he said to his papa.

"Then don't. Just put it down, son." Hank stepped

forward with one metal foot.

"Stay back!" Luke yelled.

"Give me the gun, Luke." Hank advanced again.

"Go back!" Luke screamed.

"Give. Me. The gun." Hank strode forward, abandoning all wariness. He grasped the barrel of the rifle, and was about to yank it from Luke's hands.

Then Luke pulled the trigger.

The blast covered them for a moment in a little cloud of smoke. It hid Luke's stream of tears and the shaking of his hands. It hid the blood rolling down his father's chest.

Hank looked down at the wound, then back at Luke. "You shot me."

"I didn't wanna," Luke sobbed.

"You shot ..." Hank didn't finish his sentence. He stumbled back a pace, then collapsed to the ground. That armour-piercing round was enough to kill both parts of him. No one, human or construct, could escape death.

Mrs. Mayfield ran to her husband, shrieking as she went. Nox wasn't sure if it was because he was her spouse or her experiment. Either way, the horror in her voice sounded real. He could see the effect it had on Luke, who looked like he was fighting the urge to run to them too.

The Iron Gunslinger, who had stood so silently watching guard over Laura, shifted in place. Luke wasn't just a boy any more. There he was, not quite ten, making his own rules, laying down the law. He didn't like it, and most law-makers didn't, but he gripped that rifle tighter, keeping his finger poised on the trigger.

"Wait," Mrs. Mayfield told the Iron Gunslinger, holding out her hand towards it. Nox knew it was too close. If it charged, Luke would barely have time to swing the gun around to fire. And unlike his father, one shot wouldn't count so much. They say everyone has a bullet with their name on it. The Iron Gunslinger needed a whole barrel full.

Mrs. Mayfield looked at her son with a faceful of tears. It was better, perhaps, than a faceful of lead. She shook her head in admonishment, as if her little boy had grown up to be a terrible disappointment. Not that she was there in recent months to see him grow.

"Let sis go," Luke said, choking on the words. The tears didn't make them slide out any easier. "Let Nox go." And, when his mother didn't respond. "Let them go, mama."

Mrs. Mayfield rose up, letting her husband's hand slip through hers, then clatter off the cold, cracked earth. The tears were still wet on her cheeks, but no new ones came now.

"I could crush you," she whispered. She flicked the fingers of her right hand. "Just like that."

Luke's eyes were drawn by the shifting of the Iron Gunslinger, by the grinding of its metal claws as they formed into fists.

"It would be so easy," his mother said. "So quick."

Nox watched Luke's reaction as she spoke. More than anything, he watched the position of the boy's index finger on the trigger. Instead of getting closer, it moved farther away. Nox shook his head. Luke wasn't going to shoot.

Chapter Forty-four

RUST IN THE CHAMBER

Luke threw the rifle towards the Coilhunter. It clattered off his chest, then landed a few feet away. Nox looked at the kid, incredulous. The constructs still held him down. He couldn't catch the gun, let alone fire it.

Then some of the constructs clambered off him, reaching their rusty fingers out for the weapon. It left one of his legs free, which was just in reach to kick the weapon farther away. In the process, he saw something he didn't expect: another construct parked near Oddcopper, winding him back up. So Nox struggled even more with his captors, kicking another one off with his boot.

Luke ran.

"Get him!" Mrs. Mayfield screamed.

The Iron Gunslinger bounded after him, making the ground tremor. Luke ran to his sister in her iron cage. His hand grazed hers, and then the Iron Gunslinger's fist came down upon them. He ducked, and Laura backed away. The blow left a hole in the cage.

Luke ran again, this time past Oddcopper and the other construct, which looked like a radio perched on a thin torso, with two wheels, one large and one small, beneath. It feigned death as the Iron Gunslinger came close, slumping its arms forward just like Oddcopper.

Luke ran straight for the Coilhunter, still buried beneath so many constructs. He leapt over Nox, his foot clipping the head of one of the creatures. Then the Iron Gunslinger came, and many of the other constructs baulked in its presence, abandoning their positions. Some that stayed were bowled over in the larger fiend's advance.

Nox cast off the few remaining foes and got to his feet. He instinctively reached for his belt, but there was nothing there. No gadgets. No guns. What was the Coilhunter without them? He knew he'd find out soon enough.

The surviving constructs came for him again, but he shoved them off. Some crowded around Mrs. Mayfield like a moving shield. She yelled and taunted, and it almost seemed like she was in some kind of communication, calling for more. That was the last thing Nox needed right now.

As he hauled a construct off his shoulder, tearing one of its arms off in the process, he saw Oddcopper power up again. He watched the little construct spin into action, glance at the empty ground where he had previously tried to reach the rifle, then search around to find it. Once he did, he charged forward, picking up the gun. He looked at Nox, still struggling with the leaping constructs, and then at Laura, who had just escaped through the hole in her cage. She reached her hand out for the rifle, then yanked it from Oddcopper's grasp. She hadn't gotten the chance to make her shot before. No construct was stopping her now.

She didn't take so long to aim or fire. She knew who she had to kill, the mastermind of all of this, the one who was more a mother to machines than her and Luke. She saw the constructs crowd around her target, and saw her calling for backup. So she aimed between the gaps and fired.

Her mother howled, and the constructs seemed to howl in unison.

"Stop or I'll kill her," Laura shouted at the Iron Gunslinger. It skidded to a halt, and Luke stopped too. He looked at Laura, and then his mother, who was clutching her bleeding shoulder.

There was only one more bullet in the rifle. Even in the chaos of it all, Nox was keeping count. Laura would need to make it count too. She looked at the Coilhunter, as if she hoped he had a plan. He did.

"You could've been one of us," Mrs. Mayfield told her daughter. By rights, she should've already been. *Us* should've been a family. But Mrs. Mayfield had made a home for herself in the Rust Valley. She had plenty of other sons and daughters, even if they were all made of copper and iron.

"Tell it to back away," Laura said.

Mrs. Mayfield looked at the Iron Gunslinger. "Back away."

Laura looked at the constructs crowded around the Coilhunter. "And them."

Mrs. Mayfield beckoned them over to her, adding to her shield.

"Sooner or later," Mrs. Mayfield said, "this is

gonna happen, this mergin' of the two. If it's not me, it'll be someone else. Maybe they'll use it for the war. Or maybe, like me, they'll see it's bigger even than that."

"Not if it ends with you," Laura said.

"It doesn't end here, Laura. I'll just start over."

"No," Laura said. "You won't." She fired, and the bullet struck her mother straight between the eyes. She'd had enough practice. Her hand wasn't unsteady like Luke's was. Her conviction was unwavering.

As Mrs. Mayfield collapsed into a pool of blood, the constructs went crazy, dispersing in all directions, though most of them came for the trio of living beings that had killed their human leader.

Nox charged towards Luke, grabbing him by the waist and launching a grappling hook up to the top of a scrapyard wall. It pulled them up, even as some of the scrap came tumbling down in the process. He set the boy at the pinnacle, pointed to the copter just two streets away, which could now be reached by running along the tops of the walls.

"Run, Luke."

Laura scrambled up after them, but even as she did, the Iron Gunslinger came too. It pulled at the scrap, unsettling the uneasy support between each stray piece. Laura started to slip back down, but the Coilhunter caught her and hauled her up. Luke grabbed her hand, and the two of them began to run across the top of the wall.

But the Coilhunter didn't run. As the Iron Gunslinger threatened to tear down the path the kids were running across, Nox knew he had no other choice. He had to step back into the arena, with no gadgets and no gun. He had to face the Iron Gunslinger one last time.

Chapter Forty-five

THE LAST DRAW
OF THE IRON GUN

Nox leapt down on top of the Iron Gunslinger, knocking it to the ground. He rolled to the side, straight into another construct, knocking it down as well. The horde of constructs was smaller now, but without his guns, the Coilhunter felt smaller too. He'd always said he wasn't a warrior, and here he was fighting a whole army. He had to get it back to one-on-one.

So he fired the grappling hook at one of the other scrapyard walls, letting it grab something that looked a little precarious, like it was a support for the rest. He yanked hard, and the scrap cascaded down on top of many of the assembled constructs, burying them deep beneath. He barely waited for the hook to recoil back into the launcher before he did the same on another wall, leaving just him and the Iron Gunslinger.

The larger construct got back to its feet. It stared down the Coilhunter. He didn't stare back. Instead, he was looking around the area for something to use. His armour was gone, along with his belt and guns. For all he knew, it was buried beneath one of the mountains of junk he'd just made.

Then he saw his salvation: the bladed arm of one of the smaller constructs, reaching up through one of the scrap heaps. Nox didn't need his weapons. The whole Rust Valley was littered with them.

He ran, and the Iron Gunslinger ran, but he reached the arm first. He pulled it free from its socket and held it up like a spear, bracing for the larger construct's charge. As it bounded into him, he drove the blade forward into one of its many eyes, one of those new ones it had collected after the previous battle. In the process, he cleaved off the smaller construct that had tried to merge itself with its master, making it a little less than it was before. Yet it was still formidable.

It whacked him in the chest with the back of one of its gauntleted hands, knocking him across the way. He landed with a thud on the ground, groaning. But he didn't wait for the pain to pass. He let the adrenaline drive him, getting back to his feet, and reaching out for another piece of scrap. He threw anything he could pull free at it, though most of it just clattered off the creature's frame.

Then it charged again, and he spun out of the way, striking another eye with a metal bar he'd just acquired. The construct ground to a halt in a cloud of dust, turning slowly. Every eye it lost made it harder to find the Coilhunter, and harder to hit him too. It came once more, and he dived, smashing the bar against another iron iris.

Then he seemed to disappear entirely, as if he had those little smoke bombs he used so often. Instead, he hid inside the dust kicked up by the Iron Gunslinger's frantic charges. It turned on the spot, scouring the area for him with its two remaining eyes.

Then the Coilhunter appeared suddenly, using a saw-arm to tear through one, before he disappeared again, throwing the arm away as a distraction. The Iron Gunslinger swiped at nothing. It punched at air, sending the dust sprawling again.

The Coilhunter came again, bashing apart its final eye. It was blind, like so many of the criminals the Coilhunter faced. He couldn't use a blast of light. He had to use cold, hard iron.

Then the Iron Gunslinger felt something around one of its ankles: a wire. Nox pulled hard, bringing the construct to the ground. It sprawled there for a moment, fighting ghosts. Nox had heard of the so-called machine spirits that the tribes so often talked about. He wondered if this construct fought them now. It didn't matter. All that mattered was that it fought him.

Nox pulled another bladed arm loose from the scrap heaps and brought it to the Iron Gunslinger. He threw a few spare scraps away, letting the sounds draw the construct's attention, let it think that he wasn't there, standing over it, scrapyard spear poised to strike. He drove it in, deep between the metal plates, into its ticking heart, into the cogs and springs. He worked it like a lever, shoving and pulling, until he could hear the parts inside coming loose.

The Iron Gunslinger struggled for a moment, reaching one iron claw up, before it slumped to the ground and went entirely still. Its maker, Mrs. Mayfield, who'd made this creature as the mirror image of the Coilhunter, was gone. She wasn't there to nurse it back to health. She wasn't there to make a new one. If there was a special kind of hybrid Hell, then maybe the monster and the maker would meet there, and maybe in the fire she'd continue her work.

Chapter Forty-six

ARM'S LENGTH

But the Rust Valley had more monsters.

Even as the Iron Gunslinger stopped its struggle, more constructs flooded the area, called by the sound of battle and metal, and by Mrs. Mayfield's final summons. Not all of them were beholden to her. Not all saw the merits of the hybrid race. But most of them saw the merit in catching the Coilhunter, in tearing him apart for that little bit of metal inside.

He ran, leaping up the scrap heaps, stumbling and tumbling down, skidding across battered vehicle doors, tripping over bars and bits of wire. As he climbed, he saw the small silhouettes of the kids racing along the top of one of the next scrapyard walls, then scrambling down the side to make the final run to the copter just ahead.

He followed, feeling the pain of his injuries now, and the weight of his exhaustion. It would've been so easy to give up now, to say that he'd done his bit, that the children would make it out, and he'd stopped the secret evil of the Rust Valley. But there were other evils out there too. Who'd be there to take on those? No. He had to continue. He had to fight on.

So he gave it his all. He didn't have much else to

give. He struggled forward, letting the sight of the copter beckon him, letting the sound of the constructs behind him push him on. He fired another grappling hook, letting the mechanism do some of the work for him, helping him climb that final mountain, before he let gravity take down him down the other side.

The kids charged on in a cloud of dust, with Oddcopper and his rolling companion zig-zagging along behind them. The copter was close, but Death was close too.

Luke raced towards the copter, his satchel bobbing, his hair flying. Then a clockwork construct rose from the debris, hoisting itself up on two legs made out of piston pumps, standing tall and unsteady, as if it were on stilts. It had long, curved arms, which ended with hands made of fingers of glass, enough to stab and shred the boy to pieces. Its tiny little head, barely big enough to power its long, thin body, turned to the child, and its limbs flexed in anticipation.

Luke had propelled himself forward with so much speed that now he could barely stop. His eyes went wide, his mouth dropped, and he tried to stop, skidding in the sand before the construct. Then one of its legs came down close, and then an arm swung at him. He ducked just in time, crying out.

Laura let out a terrifying scream, like a mother lion protecting her cub, and she launched herself at the construct, leaping up at its torso and grabbing hold. Her legs dangled, and the new weight she added to the construct made it even more unsteady. It moved about, trying to balance itself, and trying to shake the girl from it. She hung on by her fingernails, screaming.

Luke clambered up and ran after them, ducking a swinging arm and dodging another. One of the glass fingers caught the edge of his cheek, and he yelped as it left a small cut. He wrapped his arms around one of its legs and tried to pull it down, but instead the creature pulled him along with it.

Then it lost its balance altogether and crashed down to the ground, laying on its back. Laura rolled off, and the construct kicked Luke away into the nearby debris. The boy cringed as he braced himself, with one arm skint, and one hand full of abrasions.

"Luke!" Laura shouted, beckoning to him.

He forced himself up and made a dash for it, past the fallen construct.

Yet, just as he did, the construct swung from the ground, and Luke saw the hand of glass approach his face. He dropped to the ground, skidding beneath the swinging arm, then clambered and crawled, slipping on a sheet of metal, and throwing himself forward, until he caught Laura's bloodied hand with his own.

They raced towards the copter, reaching one of the hatch doors. Laura pulled at the handle, but it wouldn't budge.

"Come on!" Luke cried, looking around as the construct struggled up.

"It's stuck!"

They banged at the door, hearing a mumbled response from inside.

"Open up!" they screamed in unison, leaving bloodied hand prints on the door.

They heard a clang, and then the groan of gears, followed by the creak of a door opening farther away. They glanced around, spotting Porridge's head peeking out from another hatch. They didn't know the man, but with all his bright colours in that valley of grey and black, they pretty quickly knew he wasn't with the Clockwork Commune.

"This way!" the man shrieked.

They raced inside, followed by Oddcopper and his even odder consort, barely getting in before Porridge slammed and sealed the door. Porridge yelped at the sight of the constructs, until the kids calmed him down, though even then he seemed a bag of nerves—and a bright, gaudy bag at that.

"Hurry!" the man cried, trying to lodge a box against the entrance. All of them, human and construct, helped him shove it into place.

Then the blade of a saw came through the hull, and Porridge howled even louder than before.

"We have to fly," he said.

"What about Nox?" Luke asked.

The man hesitated. "He'll find a way."

Porridge dashed across the grating and leapt into the pilot's seat. He fired the copter up, which brought the vessel into the air, slow and sluggish. The whole thing groaned and coughed, and no one, not even Porridge himself, felt it was safe to fly. Yet it wasn't safe on the ground either.

The construct that had embedded the saw into the hull lost its hold and fell to the ground, smashing apart below. The copter continued its uneasy ascent, coughing out thick plumes of smoke worse than the

Coilhunter's mask. It spluttered and rumbled, and the rivets seemed about to pop.

"There!" Luke shouted, pointing through one of the bubble windows at Nox limping down below. "We need to land. We've gotta get him!"

"We can't land now," Porridge said.

"Then crash," Laura said. She didn't know that for this vessel, that meant pretty much the same thing.

Porridge looked at them with eyes that said he wasn't entirely sure he believed what he was about to say. "He'll find a way."

And Nox did.

He fired the grapnel up one last time. It grasped on, but it was an uneasy hold. The wire wound tight, pulling him up. Luke and Laura opened one of the other doors and reached out to haul him in.

Yet the Coilhunter had barely got inside when one of the copter's engines conked out. The whole vessel tumbled in the sky, sending all of them rolling around inside, all except Porridge in his track-locked chair. As they tumbled, and as the next engine kicked in and new propellers powered up to lift them all again, the door swung wide, and out fell Luke.

Chapter Forty-seven

THE LITTLE THINGS
THAT COUNT

Nox grabbed the boy's arm as he slipped down. Luke swung for a moment, yelping as his satchel slid off his shoulder. He tried to catch it with his other arm, then with his foot, but he ended up just kicking it away. It fell to the ground, the strap flapping against the breeze. Luke was lucky he didn't fall down after it. Nox pulled him up.

"My satchel," the child said.

"Leave it."

"But my drawings."

You'd think after all they'd been through, that would've been the last thing on his mind. That was until what the boy said next.

"They're all I have left of 'em."

Nox knew what he meant. He'd seen those family pictures. He had one of his own, back in his hideout, though it was taken by Five-pence Tully many years before. It didn't seem like Luke had one of those pictures, drawn by the hand of light. He had to make do with a drawing of his own.

So, Nox rolled his eyes, and rolled up his sleeves. "Wait here," he ordered.

He yanked the grappling hook from his right arm, latching it onto one of the firmer parts of the copter's interior, tugging the wire to make sure it was taut. Then he leapt outside, letting his weight unravel the cord. He swung for a moment, until one of the natural dips of the copter brought him close to the ground. He reached his other arm down and snatched up the satchel.

He could hear the shrill cries of Porridge up above as he asked the kids what the Coilhunter was doing. He could also hear the scurrying and ticking of a horde of constructs far behind him. No matter how many of them he gunned down, there were always more. He supposed they weren't that different to men after all.

He pulled down hard, which normally triggered the mechanism for the wire's recoil, but it didn't work. He tried again, looking across at the advancing wall of mismatched metal. He put the satchel around his shoulder, then tried to climb up the wire. He was glad he was wearing gloves, because it dug deep into his skin.

He was about halfway up when the horde arrived below him, clamouring in their own iron tongue. He was just about to think of how good it was that he wasn't down there with them when he felt a sudden drop. The copter had made another dip, and he was now just inches above the clamps and cleavers, the scoops and saws. He felt the edge of something sharp nick his boot.

"Up!" he yelled to the open door, barely seeing Luke and Laura scrambling about inside. He heard them shouting that same word to Porridge. "Up! Up!"

But shouting didn't help. The copter dipped down again, forcing Nox to pull up his legs as high as he could. Then it rose, and he straightened up again, just enough to scramble up the wire a little more, right before it dove again. Each time it dropped, it seemed like it went down further, as if that makeshift copter couldn't help but make the Rust Valley its bed.

It got so bad that Nox had to kick at the mangled limbs that reached out for him, sometimes knocking the poorly-soldered arms off into the distance. Yet he couldn't kick at everything. The spinning blades of saws came ever closer by the second.

Finally, he heard two new engines powering up, which set more propellers in motion. The copter ascended fast, leaving behind the constructs, who would have to wait for some other poor souls to wander into their rusty web.

Nox climbed the remainder of the wire and hauled himself inside, aided by Luke and Laura's arms. He rolled onto his back, almost flinching at the metallic clang of his oxygen tank. He held up the satchel like a trophy.

"Thanks," Luke said, taking the bag.

"Any time," Nox replied. "Well. Just this time." He took a deep breath. "Let's not come here again."

Luke sat against one of the nets, holding his little journal open. Nox didn't need to look to know what page. Laura wandered over and sat down next to him, putting her arm around his shoulder. She stared at the pencil drawing of her and Luke, with their parents on either side.

"I killed them," Luke said softly.

"No," Laura replied. "I killed them too."

"They were dead a long time ago," Nox said. "At least inside, where it counts. What you saw were just the empty shells." That's what he told himself about so many people in the Wild North. He knew it'd make it easier, because it made it easier for him. The criminals of that region were just a kind of walking dead, biding their time till he prepared their grave.

Luke looked up at the Coilhunter with that same look he'd seen in the eyes of most who'd just taken their first life. The problem with taking another's life is that it took a little part of you too.

"The memories fade," Nox said. And they did. Even the good ones.

Laura pulled her brother closer and kissed him on the forehead. "We can make new ones," she said. She didn't have that look of a first kill. She'd killed before, when the bandits came. She'd gotten it out of her system. Something about her love for her brother made up for all those little missing chips. They say a bit of love goes a long way. It stopped you becoming a shell of your own.

Nox never told the boy the entire truth, that the memories might fade, but the dreams never really did. His old battles were over, but he kept reliving them every night. That's when he felt the fire burn again, hotter than it had ever been. But maybe, just maybe, there was a little bit of healing in what you did in the day.

Chapter Forty-eight

BACK TO CIVILISATION

The Coilhunter thanked Porridge for his help, and gave him a little gift for his troubles: those two little constructs, who'd feel right at home among the scrap of the trader's copter. Oddcopper had a mate, but she needed a name. So, Laura gave her one. She called her Bitnickel.

Porridge dropped them off just outside of Lambert's Reach, due north of the Rust Valley. It was a small town, but they weren't looking for big. They were looking for something that wasn't surrounded by metal. Lambert's Reach was mostly wood.

Yet, despite all they'd been through, it didn't take long for Nox to get that sour taste back in his mouth. He saw the locals eyeing him up something dirty. They were back in civilisation, though there wasn't much civilised about it. The Northfolk used that term derisively for the south, "the so-called Civilised South." There wasn't much civilised about that either.

Nox didn't have many coils on him, but the townsfolk recognised him, and knew he wouldn't have any problem getting more. They didn't so much as trust as fear him. Even now, when he looked bruised and bloodied. In fact, that only made them fear him more.

"Where'd you come from?" Looselip Lambert asked. He was a man of gossip, looking for a new story more than a handful of coils. You see, the coils always ran out. But the stories stayed.

"The Rust Valley," Nox said.

"You're kiddin'."

"Do I look like I'm kiddin'?"

"You look like you barely got out."

"Barely's fine by me," Nox said. "It's better than most."

"And the kids?" Lambert pointed to the duo behind him.

"None of your business."

"Well, I'm puttin' my trust in you here. If you want the wagon, it'll cost double the normal rate."

"Let's make it triple. For your trouble. And your silence."

"Well, then. How can I say no to that?"

Nox forced a smile with his eyes. "You can't."

They stayed the night there, in a room above the bar, with Lambert's best hospitality. His daughter brought them food and drink, and helped them mend their wounds. Nox knew he'd receive a bill for that as well.

Laura went out like a light, but Luke had trouble sleeping. Nox knew he was starting to have his own nightmares too. Exhaustion was no defence against them. They, like the land, would get you anywhere.

"It gets better," Nox told him between one of his own restless dozes.

Luke handed him a piece of paper he'd torn out of

his sacred journal. Nox held it up. It was the drawing of him, but now it was finished. He didn't draw all the cuts and bruises. He drew him all patched up and perfect. If only the reality matched.

"It's yours," the boy said.

"You keep it," Nox replied. "To remember me."

"I don't need it to remember you."

They left just before dawn, before most of the townsfolk could gather. It was better to let Lambert tell them the story. Nox didn't want to tell it himself.

As Nox loaded up the wagon, he passed a girl sticking her tongue out at a boy on the porch. Their mother was there too, sweeping the streets. They were the only ones out there, the early risers, just like him. They didn't take any notice, because the slivers of dawnlight hadn't yet shown Nox's distinctive mask.

"No, you're a construct," the girl said. They pushed and shoved, and giggled. The parents watched on, full of chuckles of their own.

To them, to all of them, it was just a game. None of them really knew what was out there in the Rust Valley. Even the sun looked away. They looked to the here and now, and maybe that was how you stayed sane. None of them looked to what might be coming, what might be coming for all of them. But Nox did. And he thought he best prepare for it.

Chapter Forty-nine

HOME

The Coilhunter didn't so much have a home as a hideout, a place to recover between each chase and kill. It was his workshop, where he made his dangerous toys. But it wasn't home, and he knew it could never be a home to Luke and Laura. He was dangerous too. They'd be safer if they weren't associated with him, away from the vendettas of the Wild North's gangs.

So he had to look somewhere else. He knew a lot of people, but few were good. One name came to mind.

Sally Hays.

She was better known as Handcart Sally. When he arrived at her new ranch up north, just bordering tribal territory, he couldn't quite believe his eyes. Boy, she was the same as she ever was. Her hair fell in perfect waves upon her shoulders, all gold and crisp. Though she hadn't touched a mine in years, she somehow still seemed to get soot on her face, or maybe she just couldn't get it out. She didn't bother with lipstick and eyeliner, and she didn't have to. She kept the sun at bay with her wide-brimmed straw hat.

She stood there, not moving, linking her thumbs

through the belt loops of her jeans. The sun gave her a pleasant glow. It wasn't so kind to the rest of them. Beside her, munching the few stray bits of grass, was a mighty stallion, with its golden mane made to rival Sally's.

Nox left the kids in the wagon and strolled up. Even when he concentrated, he found it hard to hide that gunslinger's gait. He wasn't trying to be intimidating. The days of chasing Handcart Sally across the desert were over. Now, he always knew where to find her.

"Well, look who it is," Sally said. "Ain't that a sight for sore eyes."

Nox tipped his hat. "Been a while."

"So it has. Why, if I didn't keep seein' posters disappearin' off o' buildings, I'd have thought you were dead."

"You know me. Always trudging on."

"I do indeed."

Nox ran his hand down the horse's mane. "You finally did it."

She smirked. "A girl can dream."

"A girl can do anything she wants."

They both smiled in silence for a moment.

"What's his name?" Nox asked, patting the horse again. He was a gentle animal, too tame for the Wild North. Nox wondered if it was Sally's influence that did that. She had a way of taming things.

Sally combed her fingers through the horse's mane on the other side, bringing her hand up closer to Nox's each time, though never close enough. "Old-timer Bill."

"By the sounds of it, he ain't new."

"He's not, though you wouldn't think it by the looks of 'im. He's twenty-five now."

"That so? 'Bout the average lifespan of folk up here."

"Oh, I think it's less than that," Sally said. "But Old-timer Bill should live to sixty, even with the heat. He's one of those shadow mustangs from the Losa Ariasa. Got 'im for a good price too."

"The Dust Riders? Why'd they part with him?"

"I've got an Ootana friend."

Nox raised an eyebrow. "Don't we all?"

"Well, they might say they're at peace with everyone, but for some of us, they really mean it." She grasped the feather hanging from her necklace and rolled it between her fingers. Nox knew that symbol well. The feather of the tamba bird, a sign of peace.

"And the other tribes didn't object?"

"Hell if I know. But so what if they do? I've got the Ariasa license. It's as good as your posters. Better, even. But I think if they didn't like it, they'd have said so by now—probably with arrows. I've had Oldtimer Bill now for almost two years. I've put my stamp on 'im, so I have. He's got the old Sally spirit in 'im."

"So long as it ain't Handcart Sally spirit."

She frowned. "It ain't. You know those days are behind me now."

Nox said nothing. You could never really get a clean slate, even though many came to the Wild North for just that. She couldn't shake the name Handcart Sally any more than he could shake all those names the Northfolk had for him. Every so often he still saw her face on a poster for some old crime, but now things were different. Now he pulled those posters down.

They stared at each other over the horse's mane. It was always easier when there was something between them. Most times it was the great expanse of the desert. It was easier that way—except on the lonely nights. The bodies of criminals weren't great company.

"He's a good horse," Nox said eventually, pulling away from her gaze.

"You should get yourself one. I could put in a good word."

"I'll stick with the iron equivalent, I think. Suits me just fine."

"I heard you lost yours though. Monowheels ain't exactly easy to come by. I don't got any connections for that."

"I won't need them. I'll build a new one."

"It's good how you can do that."

"We all can, in our own way."

"Build a new life," Sally mused. "Ain't no blueprint for that."

"I guess not."

"So, what brings you here?" She peered over his shoulder at the cart far off down the road. "I'd wager you didn't come in something that big if you were on your lonesome."

"You'd wager right," Nox said.

"What's the matter?"

"I need a favour. A big one."

"Most favours are, in their own way."

"Well, this is bigger than most."

"Spill."

"You wanted a family, right?"

"Yeah," she said, "but I can't have one now. Not if I don't want no demon spawn."

"That's a myth."

"That's easy for a man to say."

"Well, what about if the kids are already born?"

"Huh?"

"I mean, what if there were two orphans out there, lookin' for a home."

"I'd ask where your home is," Sally said, "but I know you don't got one."

"I'm serious," Nox said.

"I know you are. When were you anything but?"

"If you've got room, I've got two who could do with it."

Sally stared at the wagon, where Laura and Luke peered out.

"That's askin' a lot."

"I know."

"Not just of me. Of them too."

"I know."

She rubbed her hand across her mouth. He thought he saw it tremor a little before she hid it with her fingers. She looked at him. "A family," she said, her voice hushed. Nox knew that was something she always wanted, but never had. It was what he wanted too, though he'd already had it once. It was easier to be alone. That way you couldn't lose anyone but yourself.

"I'll do it," she said. "On one condition."

"Name it."

"You visit."

"That's probably not wise."

"Maybe it's not, but that's my line in the sand."

"It'd have to be a big line," Nox said, gesturing to the vastness of the desert.

"It is."

He sighed. "Well, okay then. I'll visit."

"Or, y'know, you could stay."

They locked eyes for a moment, like they had so many times before, and then he looked away, back to the endless desert.

"You could have your life back," she told him, though it sounded like she only half believed it. "You could have … a family."

He stifled a sigh, hiding the jitter of his breath. He was glad the hot desert air dried up his eyes. Whatever words he was trying to find caught in his throat. He glanced at the girl and boy, staring out of the wagon. He turned away again, just as he had turned away from the memories of past glances at his own little Ambrose and Aaron. He'd already told Luke and Laura about Sally, and that he wasn't staying—that he couldn't stay. They got out now and stood close to the cart.

Sally reached her delicate hand out, grasping the bottom of his mask, and turned his head back towards her.

"Don't you want this?" she asked.

"I want this," he said, a shudder in his voice. "But I can't have it."

"Why can't you?"

"Because if I take this, then they'll win."

Sally frowned. "Doesn't that mean then that you'll always lose?"

"It ain't about me."

"But why ain't it? Don't you think you matter? Don't you think you deserve some happiness?"

"Maybe I do, but so do a lot of people in these here parts. They'll never have it so long as the gangs get their way. What's one man's happiness compared to that of a hundred?"

"Everything," Sally said, "to the man."

"Well, we all got to make sacrifices."

"Seems like you're makin' 'em all."

"Why, that makes me sound more important than I am. There's other good men out there too. Not many of 'em, but they're out there. And for the rest, well, I make 'em take sacrifices too."

"You won't let this life o' yours go, will you?" Sally asked.

"You've got it wrong," he replied, shaking his head. "It won't let me go."

He turned to leave, but his heart made him look back. He saw Sally there, then turned to see Laura far behind at the wagon, with her hands on Luke's shoulders. The boy waved slowly, sadly. This was why he didn't want to know their names.

He turned back to the unmarked paths of the sand, and pulled a poster out of his pocket, rolled up next to the drawing Luke had made. The poster had a different name: *Lawless Lyle*. It'd help him forget the others. Just as much as his heart panged, his fingers itched. He felt the soft sand beneath his feet, and his pistols at his hips. He walked on, letting the sun hound him and the wind lead him. He knew he wouldn't have to walk far before he'd find his next destination, and yet another name for his list.

ABOUT THE AUTHOR

Dean F. Wilson was born in Dublin, Ireland in 1987. He started writing at age 11, and has since become a *USA Today* and *Wall Street Journal* Bestselling Author.

He is the author of the *Children of Telm* epic fantasy trilogy, the *Great Iron War* steampunk series, the *Coilhunter Chronicles* science-fiction western series, the *Hibernian Hollows* urban fantasy series, and the *Infinite Stars* space opera series.

Dean previously worked as a journalist, primarily in the field of technology. He has written for *TechEye*, *Thinq*, *V3*, *VR-Zone*, *ITProPortal*, *TechRadar Pro*, and *The Inquirer*.

www.deanfwilson.com

Made in the USA
Middletown, DE
24 July 2021

44724897R00139